THE BABY-SITTERS CLUB

Kristy and the Snobs

Ann M. Martin

AN
APPLE
PAPERBACK

D0125679

SCHOLASTIC INC.
New York Toronto London Auckland Sydney

ISBN 0-590-41125-X

Copyright © 1988 by Ann M. Martin. All rights reserved. Published by Scholastic Inc. APPLE PAPERBACKS is a registered trademark of Scholastic Inc. THE BABY-SITTERS CLUB is a trademark of Scholastic Inc.

12 11 10 9 8 7 6 5 4   8 9/8 0 1 2 3/9

Printed in the U.S.A.   11

First Scholastic printing, March 1988

In memory of Neena and Grandpa

CHAPTER 1

If there's one thing I can't stand, it's a snob. Well, actually, there are a lot of other things I can't stand. Cabbage, blood, people who chew with their mouths open, and squirrels are a few of them. But snobs are way up there on the list.

This is unfortunate since I have moved to a wealthy neighborhood here in Stoneybrook, Connecticut, recently, and it is overrun with snobs. What happened was that my mom, who used to be divorced, got remarried to Watson Brewer, this rich guy. Since my mom had a little house for the six of us (Mom, me, my three brothers, and our dog, Louie), and Watson had this mansion all to himself (his two kids only live with him every other weekend), it made more sense for us Thomases to move in with Watson than for him to move in with us.

So we did.

1

Watson's house is so big that my brothers and I, and Karen and Andrew (our stepsister and stepbrother, who live with us every other weekend), each have a room of our own. Mom and Watson share a room, of course, but their "room" is really a suite about the size of a landing field.

Anyway, to get back to the snobs — I'm surrounded. They're everywhere in Watson's neighborhood. The teenagers around here get their own cars (fancy ones) as soon as they're able to drive. They spin along with the radios blaring, looking fresh and sophisticated. I am *so glad* my big brothers, Sam and Charlie, aren't like that. Charlie can drive now, but the only thing he drives is Mom's beat-up station wagon. And my brothers and I still go to public school, not to snobby private schools. Guess what most families on our street have: (a) a swimming pool (b) tennis courts (c) a cook named Agnes (d) all of the above. The answer is (d) all of the above.

So far, Watson has (e) none of the above, which is one of the things I'm learning to like about him. However, he's been talking about putting in a pool, now that Karen and Andrew are older, so we'll see.

I've hardly gotten to know any of the kids here. When we first moved into Watson's house it was summertime, the beginning of July. Most of the kids my age had been sent to fancy camps for the summer. (I would kill Mom if she ever did that to me.) Plus, I'm president of a group called the Baby-sitters Club. All my friends are in the club, and they live way across town — where I used to live — so I spent a lot of time with them over in my old neighborhood last summer. What I'm trying to say is that school had started again before I met any of the kids on my street.

My first encounter with the snobby kids was on a Monday morning. My alarm clock went off at 6:45 as usual. I rolled over and tried to ignore it.

"Please, please be quiet," I mumbled.

But the clock didn't obey. It went right on buzzing.

"Oh, all right, you win," I told it.

I reached over and shut it off, then sat up, rubbing my eyes.

"Louie!" I exclaimed. Our old collie was stretched across the foot of my big bed. Louie mostly sleeps with David Michael, but lately, he's been taking turns sleeping with all of us, even Karen and Andrew on the weekends they visit. I thought it was nice of Louie to share himself.

"You are such a good dog," I whispered, leaning over to him. I stroked the top of his head between his ears. The fur there is almost as soft as rabbit fur. Then I took one of his paws in my hand.

"Oh, your pads are cold," I told him, rubbing the pink pads on the bottom of his paw. "It must be getting chilly at night. Poor old Louie."

Louie licked my hand and gave me a doggie smile.

"Thanks," I said.

I got up and looked through my closet, as if I had a really big decision to make about what to wear. Ever since school began I've been wearing the same kind of outfit almost every day — a turtleneck, a sweater, jeans, and sneakers. I don't care about clothes the way my friends Claudia and Stacey do. They always look really cool and put-together.

After I was washed and dressed, I ran down the wide staircase to the first floor and into the kitchen. Mom and Watson were with Sam and Charlie. (David Michael, my seven-year-old brother, is a slowpoke. He's always the last one down.)

Here's another thing about Watson that's not so bad. He helps out around the house — with the cooking, cleaning, gardening, everything. I guess this comes from being divorced and having lived alone for awhile before he met Mom. He and Mom share the workload equally. They both have jobs, they both prepare meals (Watson is actually a better cook than Mom is), they both run errands, etc. Twice a week, a cleaning lady comes in, and my brothers and I are responsible for certain chores, but basically Mom and Watson run the show.

So I wasn't surprised when I stepped into the kitchen that Monday morning to find Mom making coffee and Watson scrambling eggs. Sam was setting the table and Charlie was pouring orange juice. It was a nice familiar scene.

"Good morning!" I said.

"Morning," everyone replied.

"Kristy, can't you wear something different once in awhile?" Sam asked me, eyeing my jeans and sweater.

"Why do you care what I wear?" I replied, but I knew perfectly well why he cared. He cared because he was fifteen and girls were practically the only thing on his mind. He thought he was the girl expert of the world, and he was disappointed in my lack of fashion sense. Plus, he was interested in this *très* sophisticated girl down the street (one of the private-school girls) and he wanted everything about our family to be up to Monique's standards, which were sky-high.

"I think Kristy looks lovely," said Watson.

"So do I," added Mom, kissing the top of my head.

"But," Watson went on, "if you ever do want a few, um, new clothes, all you have to do is holler."

It was a nice offer, but leave it to Watson to use a word like "holler."

"Thanks," I said. "I'll remember that."

I absolutely adore Watson's kitchen. Although it has all the modern conveniences and appliances, it looks kind of like an old country kitchen. We eat at a big parson's table with two long benches. (Watson and Mom bought it when they got married.) Most of the counter tops are covered with blue and white tiles. Copper pots and pans hang from the walls. The curtains — tiny pink and blue flowers on a cream-colored background — match the wallpaper. It's a wonderful, cozy room.

I plopped down on one of the benches, and almost at once Mom said, "Kristy, call David Michael, please, honey."

"DAVID MICHAEL!" I yelled.

"*Kristy*," said Mom, giving me a look that was part smile, part exasperation.

"I know, I know." I got up, went to the

bottom of the stairs, and called him again.

"Kristy, can you come up here?" he replied.

I ran up the stairs and into his room. "What?" I asked.

David Michael was sitting on the floor next to Louie. "Call Louie," he said.

"Why?" I asked.

"Just call him."

I got down on one knee. "Louie! Come here, boy!" I clapped my hands.

Louie hobbled toward me. He was limping. "Hmm," I said. "I see what you mean."

"I looked at all his paws," David Michael told me, "but I can't find any cuts or insect bites or burrs."

"Poor old Louie," I said for the second time that day. "Well, don't worry, David Michael. We'll tell Mom, but it's probably nothing."

I should mention here that although we got Louie right after I was born, he's really more David Michael's dog than anyone else's. We all love Louie, but David Michael has especially loved him, even as a baby, and he's always taken care of him. He's never complained about messy dog food cans or smelly flea collars. It was David Michael who discovered a rock song called "Brother Louie." (That's the one that goes "Louie, Louie, Louie, Lou-*ee*.") Whenever he plays it, the real Louie howls joyfully each time he hears his name. One of David Michael's very first words was even "Yew-ee." (Louie still responds if someone calls him that.) And Louie has always loved David Michael right back. Maybe he somehow sensed that David Michael was the only one of us Thomas kids who got cheated out of a father, since Mom and Dad got separated not long after David Michael was born. Who knows?

Louie followed David Michael and me down the stairs and into the kitchen. "Mom," I said, "Louie's limping," but already his limp seemed less noticeable.

"I guess so," Mom said slowly, watching him. "It's hard to tell. We'll keep our eyes on him."

As soon as breakfast was over, things became hectic. Charlie and Sam got in the station wagon and left for the high school. Mom and Watson drove off, in separate cars, to their jobs. And David Michael and I waited at the end of the drive for our school buses. It was only 7:45, but I felt like I'd been up forever.

David Michael's bus was right on time. He climbed on and waved good-bye to me from a window in the very back. He loves to sit in the backseat. My bus should have been just behind David Michael's, but it wasn't. By 7:55, it was later than it had ever been. It better hurry, I thought. Homeroom starts at 8:30. Sharp.

For awhile I worried about what to do if the bus didn't come at all. Call Stacey's house? Stacey's mom was one of the few I knew who didn't work and might be at home. Then I wondered how long I should wait before I called anybody.

Before I reached any decisions, something interesting happened. The front door of a house across the street opened and a girl about my age stepped out. She was carrying a knapsack, and wearing a blue plaid jumper over a white short-sleeved blouse. She walked down her driveway and stood across the street from me. She must have been waiting for a bus, too, but not mine. I was the only girl in this neighborhood who got picked up by the bus to Stoneybrook Middle School.

The girl and I eyed each other, but didn't say anything.

A few minutes later, three other girls joined the first one. They were all wearing the exact same outfit — a private-school uniform. They were slender, three of them had blonde hair, and they were wearing makeup and stockings. They looked sleek, sophisticated, and self-confident. They stood in a huddle, whispering and giggling. Every now and then one of them would glance over at me.

Where, oh, where was my bus?

I tried not to look at the girls. I pretended the cover of my notebook was absolutely fascinating.

But the girls would not allow me to ignore them. One of the blondes, who wore her hair in a cascade of thick curls, called to me, "You're Mr. Brewer's new kid, aren't you?"

"I'm one of them," I replied warily.

"Are you the one who's been sending those fliers around? For some baby-sitting club?"

"Yeah," I said. (Every now and then our club tries to find new people to baby-sit for, so we send around advertisements. We'd put one in every box in my new neighborhood not long ago.)

"What does your little club do?" asked another blonde.

"What do you think?" I replied testily. "We baby-sit."

"How cute," said the blonde with the curls.

The others giggled.

"Nice outfit," called the one non-blonde, putting her hands on her hips.

I blushed. Too bad I'd chosen the jeans with the hole in the knee that day.

But if there's one thing to be said about me, it's that I have a big mouth. I always have. I'm better about controlling it than I used to be, but I'm not afraid to use it. So I put *my* hands on *my* hips and said, "Your outfits are nice, too. You look like clones. Snob clones."

Luckily, just at that moment, my bus finally pulled up. I chose a seat on the side of the bus facing the girls. I lowered my window. "Good-bye, snobs," I shouted.

" 'Bye, jerk-face," the curly-haired blonde replied.

I stuck my tongue out at her, and then the bus turned a corner and they were gone from sight.

CHAPTER 2

"Thanks, Charlie! See you later! 'Bye!" I slammed the car door.

Charlie backed down the Kishis' driveway as I ran to their front door and rang the bell. It was time for our Monday afternoon meeting of the Baby-sitters Club.

Janine Kishi, Claudia's older sister, answered the door. Janine has never been one of my favorite people, but lately she's seemed a little better than usual. The thing about Janine is that she's *so smart*. She's always correcting everybody.

But that day, all she said was, "Come on in. Claudia's upstairs. Dawn and Mary Anne are there, too."

"Thank you," I replied politely. But I didn't go straight upstairs. I stopped in the kitchen to say hello to Mimi, Claudia's grandmother. Mimi had a stroke over the summer, but she's getting much better. She can't use her right hand, so she's learning to do things one-handed. When I looked in on her, she was stirring something at the stove.

"Hi, Mimi," I greeted her.

"Kristy. Hello. How nice to see." Mimi's native language is Japanese, and her speech was affected by the stroke, so she has a little trouble speaking. "How things in your new neighborhood?"

"Okay, I guess. I don't know that many people." For some reason, I was embarrassed to tell her what had happened at the bus stop that morning.

"You will get to know new people," Mimi told me confidently. "That I am sure."

"Thanks," I said and ran upstairs. On the way I heard the doorbell ring. It must have been Stacey. Good. She was right on time. The five of us could begin our meeting.

"Hi, you guys!" I called as I entered Claudia's room.

"Hi!" Claudia, Dawn, and Mary Anne were lying on the floor, looking through our club notebook. When Stacey came in behind me, the five of us scrambled for places to sit. Claudia dove for the bed, followed by Stacey. Dawn and Mary Anne remained on the floor, and I settled myself in the director's chair, put on my visor, and stuck a pencil behind one ear. I always get the director's chair.

I am the president.

I looked at the other members of the Baby-sitters Club: Claudia Kishi, Mary Anne Spier, Stacey McGill, and Dawn Schafer. All present. I guess I should introduce them. But first I should tell you how our club works. We hold meetings on Mondays, Wednesdays, and Fridays from five-thirty until six, and our clients know they can reach us at Claudia's house then. They call when they need sitters, and one of us signs up for the job. Simple. Our clients like the fact that they're pretty much guaranteed a sitter when they call, and we like all the jobs we get. Of course, we have an awful lot of clients now (we've been in business for a year), and sometimes we're so busy that none of us is able to take on a job. Then we call Logan Bruno. Logan is our associate member, sort of our safety. He doesn't come to meetings, but he likes to baby-sit. He's also Mary Anne's boyfriend.

The club officers are our vice-president, Claudia; our secretary, Mary Anne; our treasurer, Stacey; and our alternate officer, Dawn. Claudia was chosen as vice-president since she has her own personal telephone and phone number. Because of that, we decided to hold our meetings in her room. Claudia works hard for the club, since she has to take a lot of job calls that come in while we're not having meetings. Here are the essentials about Claudia: Likes — art, mysteries, baby-sitting, boys. Dislikes — school. Looks — beautiful, Japanese, exotic. Dress — *very* trendy and cool, often outrageous. Personality — outgoing, sometimes feels inferior to Janine. (Who wouldn't?)

Mary Anne, our secretary, is my best friend. Before I moved to Watson's we lived next door to each other for years and years. We were babies, kids, and almost teenagers together. Right now, Mary Anne is changing. I think she's growing up a little faster than I am. And she has another best friend (Dawn). We're alike in a lot of ways and different in a lot of ways. For instance, my likes — sports, baby-sitting, TV. Mary Anne's likes — baby-sitting, movie stars, animals. My dislikes — you already know them. Mary Anne's dislikes — crowds of people, being the center of attention. Looks — we're both small for our age, and we both have brown eyes and medium-length brown hair. Dress — I couldn't care less. Mary Anne is just beginning to care, but she needs a lot of help from Claudia and Stacey. My personality —

outgoing, big mouth, friendly. Mary Anne's personality — cautious, sensitive, shy. (She has a boyfriend. I don't.) Mary Anne's club job is to keep our record book up to date. The record book is where we write down our clients' names, addresses, and phone numbers, list the money we earn (that's really Stacey's job), and most important, schedule our baby-sitting jobs.

Stacey McGill is sort of a newcomer to Stoneybrook. Until a year ago, she and her parents lived in New York City. They moved here just before we began school last September. Stacey is sophisticated and smart. Sometimes she seems years older than me. She and Claudia are best friends. Stacey's likes — boys, clothes, baby-sitting. Dislikes — doctors. (Stacey has diabetes and has to go to doctors pretty often. She also dislikes the strict diet she has to stay on so as not to allow too much sugar in her body.) Looks — wild blonde hair, thin, pretty, older than her age. Dress — as trendy as Claudia, but a little less outrageous. Personality — outgoing, very grown-up, sensitive to other people. Stacey keeps track of the earnings of us baby-sitters, and is responsible for the dues we put in our club treasury.

Finally, there's Dawn, who's more of a newcomer to Stoneybrook than Stacey is. She moved here from California last January with her mother and younger brother after her parents got divorced. Dawn's job as alternate officer is to take over the duties of any other officer if someone gets sick or has to miss a meeting. Dawn's likes — health food, sunshine, baby-sitting, ghost stories. Dislikes — junk food, cold weather. Looks — the longest, palest, shini-est, silkiest blonde hair you can imagine. Dress — whatever she feels like. Dawn is an individual. Personality — confident, doesn't care what other people think of her.

And that's the five of us. Together we make a pretty good team.

I realized that my friends were looking at me, waiting for me to begin the meeting.

"The meeting will now come to order," I said, even though we already were in order. "Stacey, how much money is in the treasury?"

"Give me your weekly dues first," she replied. (Monday is Dues Day.)

Each of us handed Stacey a dollar.

"We've got nine dollars and eighteen cents," she reported.

"That's kind of low, isn't it?" I replied.

"Well, we pay Charlie to drive you to and from the meetings," said Stacey, "and we just bought coloring books and sticker books for the Kid-Kits. We're okay as long as we don't buy anything for awhile. We'll just let our dues pile up.''

(Kid-Kits are boxes filled with games and books — our old ones, mostly — plus new coloring books, crayons, activity books, etc. that we sometimes bring on baby-sitting jobs. The kids love them.)

"Anything else to report?" I asked.

The club members shook their heads.

"Have you been keeping up with the notebook?"

The club members nodded their heads — but Claudia, Dawn, and Mary Anne looked a little guilty. I knew they'd just been reading the notebook before I came into the room. We're responsible for writing up every job we go on. We record the jobs in our club notebook and then we're supposed to read the notebook each week to see what happened when our friends were baby-sitting. It's not always very interesting, but it's usually helpful.

The telephone rang then with what was probably going to be the first job of the meeting.

Dawn answered it. "Hello, Baby-sitters Club."

(See how professional we sound?)

"Okay, Mrs. Rodowsky. I'll call you right back." Dawn hung up the phone and turned to us. "Mrs. Rodowsky needs a sitter for Jackie and his brothers next Tuesday afternoon from three-thirty till six."

"Let's see," said Mary Anne, who had already turned to the appointment pages of our record book. "Claudia, you're the only one free."

"Okay," said Claudia. "I guess I can handle Jackie." (Jackie's a nice little kid, but he's accident-prone and always in trouble.)

Dawn called Mrs. Rodowsky back to tell her that Claudia would be her sitter on Tuesday.

A bunch of other calls came in then, but the most interesting one — just before the meeting came to an end — was from Mr. Papadakis. The Papadakises live not far from me in the new neighborhood. They have three kids — Linny, who's eight and a friend of David Michael; Hannie, who's six and a friend of Karen; and Sari, who's just two. I knew the Papadakises a little through David Michael and Karen, but I'd never sat for them. Now Mr. Papadakis was calling with a job.

"We saved your flier," he told me. "We need a sitter on Thursday afternoon and we know Linny and Hannie like you."

"You take the job! You take the job!" Mary Anne said excitedly to me after I'd told Mr. Papadakis I'd call him back. "You're free and it's good for you to sit in your new neighborhood."

"Well . . . okay!" I said.

At that time, I had no idea what a sitting job in my new neighborhood would really mean, and so — I was foolish enough to look forward to it.

CHAPTER 3

Charlie picked me up promptly at six o'clock and we headed back to our house. (It had been a long time before I could think of *Watson's* house as *ours*.)

"I can't wait to see how Louie's doing," I said as Charlie pulled up to a stop sign.

"Didn't you see him this afternoon?" he asked.

"I didn't have time. I stayed at school to watch a field hockey game. The late bus dropped me off just in time for you to pick me up and take me to Claudia's."

"Oh," said Charlie. "Well, I'm sure he's fine."

"I hope so," I replied.

But when we got home, Louie wasn't fine. He was resting in the living room on his orange blanket, and he didn't get up when he saw us. Usually, he's on his feet in a flash, wanting to play or to be let out.

"Hi, Louie!" I said. "Come here, boy."

Louie lifted his head off his paws, but didn't get up. I had to call him two more times before he stood up. He began to walk toward me. It was still hard to tell whether he was limping, but what nobody missed was when he walked smack into a table leg instead of my outstretched arms. David Michael and Mom had just entered the room, so they saw the whole thing, along with Charlie and me.

"Oh, Louie," murmured Mom, leaning over to pat his head. "What's wrong, boy?"

"He's not too sick," announced David Michael. "I just gave him his supper and he ate it in one gulp."

"Well," said Mom, "maybe he ought to have a check-up with Dr. Smith tomorrow. I'll call her answering service tonight and try to make an appointment. Charlie, could you take him after school?"

"Sure," replied Charlie.

"I'll go with you," I said.

"Me, too," added David Michael.

So it was arranged. The next afternoon, Charlie drove David Michael and Louie and me to Dr. Smith's office.

Louie does not like the vet. He never has. And he's pretty noisy about it. Somehow, he figures out where we're going when we're only halfway there. Then the whining starts. He can be really pathetic. David Michael is always prepared, though. He fishes doggie treats out of his pocket and feeds them to Louie one at a time.

In between bites, though, Louie whines. Charlie says it drives him crazy, but we made it to the vet without incident.

Dr. Smith's waiting room wasn't very crowded, thank goodness. There were only two patients ahead of us — a dachshund with his front paw in a cast, and a cat in a carrying case who kept yowling unhappily. Louie was well-behaved. He lay on the floor with his head resting pitifully on Charlie's shoe and whined so softly you could hardly hear him.

When Dr. Smith's assistant called for Louie Thomas, Charlie, David Michael, and I rose as one. With a lot of prodding, Louie came, too. Charlie and I hoisted him onto the metal table in the examining room.

"Hello, Thomases," Dr. Smith greeted us as she entered the room.

"Hi," we replied.

We really like Dr. Smith. She's an older woman with graying hair and bifocals who's wonderful with animals. She talks to them in a soft, soothing voice. I've never heard her raise it, not even the time Louie panicked and knocked over a box of sterile bandages.

"Well, what's wrong with Louie today?" asked the doctor.

David Michael spoke up. "We're not sure. Yesterday I thought he was limping, but it's hard to tell."

"He just lies around," I added. "And last night he walked right into a table when he was aiming for me."

"But his appetite is fine," said Charlie. "He always eats his meals."

"Well, let's have a look." Dr. Smith examined Louie carefully. She poked him and stroked him, listened to his heart, looked in his eyes and ears, and watched him try to walk. She frowned as Louie lumbered stiffly into the door jamb. Then she examined his eyes again and sort of massaged his legs.

When she was finished, she looked at us gravely.

"What is it?" I asked, suddenly feeling afraid. Awful thoughts began to run through my mind. The worst was, *Louie has cancer.*

But what Dr. Smith said was, "Louie is getting old."

My brothers and I nodded.

"And just like some old people, his body is beginning to slow down. He's developing arthritis and his eyesight is poor."

24

Is that all? I thought. Arthritis and poor eyesight? It didn't sound too bad.

"Can dogs get contact lenses?" asked David Michael seriously.

Dr. Smith smiled. "I'm afraid not, honey."

I wondered why she still looked so solemn.

"What can we do for him?" asked Charlie.

"Well, he's probably in a fair amount of pain. I can give you some pills to ease it, but they won't cure the arthritis, and the arthritis is probably going to get worse. His eyes may, too."

Now I understood. Louie was in pain. There wasn't much we could do for him and he wasn't going to get better. It wasn't as if he had a cold or an injury. I looked down at him. He had settled onto the floor of the examining room. It must be scary, I thought, not to see well and to know that you're in a strange place. No wonder Louie had walked into the side of the door.

I realized that Dr. Smith was talking again. "Please tell your mother to call me anytime if she has questions. We can strengthen the dosage of the pills if Louie seems to be worse, but I don't want to do that yet. I have a feeling Louie's got a tough road ahead of him."

David Michael was sitting on the floor, talking to Louie. I was glad he wasn't paying attention. I couldn't speak to the doctor because a lump had formed in my throat. But Charlie took over.

"We'll tell Mom," he said. "Is there anything else we can do for Louie?"

"Stairs will be difficult," replied Dr. Smith, "so keep his food and water on the level of the house where he spends the most time. Carry him up and down stairs if you can. But he *will* need a little exercise. Short, slow walks. Let him go at his own pace."

Charlie and I nodded.

"Can we leave now?" asked David Michael impatiently, and Dr. Smith laughed.

"Had enough of the doctor's office?" she asked.

"Louie has."

Dr. Smith handed a packet of pills to Charlie and explained when to give them to Louie. Then we left. Charlie and I looked as if we were on our way to a funeral. But David Michael walked Louie jauntily to the car, singing a song that he made up as he went along.

"Oh, you're going home, Louie, and you're fi–i–i–ine," he said. "No shots, no stitches, no treatment. You don't even have to spend the ni–i–i–ight."

Charlie and I glanced at each other. Obviously David Michael didn't understand that

Louie was in bad shape. All he knew was that the doctor had sent him home with some pills. How sick could he be? Pills always made David Michael better.

I felt awful by the time we reached our house. "I think I'll take Louie for a walk," I told my brothers. "A slow one, like Dr. Smith suggested." I was hoping it would calm me down.

Charlie must have guessed how I was feeling because when David Michael said, "I'll come with you!" Charlie said, "Why don't you come with me instead, kiddo? We can give your new football a workout."

I flashed Charlie a grateful smile, and Louie and I started slowly down the drive to the shady street. I remembered the day us Thomases moved into Watson's house. The morning before, we had really spruced Louie up because we'd wanted him to look his best when he came to this neighborhood, where (I was sure) all the dogs were purebred, pedigreed, and groomed at doggie parlors.

Well, that was several months ago. Since I hadn't met many of the people around here, I hadn't met many of their dogs, either. I had no idea what they were like. No question about it, though, Louie was not at his best as we plodded down the street. His head was hanging (Was he trying to see the ground better?),

27

he moved stiffly, his fur was all ruffled from the examination, and he smelled of the vet.

So wouldn't you just *know* that I'd run into that curly-haired blonde girl I'd seen at the bus stop the day before? She was flouncing down the street toward me, a leash in her hand. At the end of the leash was an absolutely gorgeous dog. It looked something like a heavy golden retriever with the markings of a Saint Bernard. And with the girl and the dog was a littler blonde, holding a spotless white Persian cat in her arms.

Our eyes met, the sidewalk was narrow, there was no way the girls and I could avoid each other.

They stopped a couple of yards away from me, and the big snob girl flipped her hair over her shoulder, and put her hand on her hip.

"What," she said, pointing to Louie, "is *that?*"

"*That*," I replied, "is a dog."

The girl made a face at me. "Really? It's hard to tell. He's so . . . scruffy."

"Yeah, he's *icky!*" cried the younger one.

"He's old," I said defensively. "And he has arthritis."

The older girl softened just a smidge. "What's his name?" she asked.

"Louie."

"Oh. This is Astrid. Astrid of Grenville. A pedigreed Bernese mountain dog."

"And *this* is Priscilla. She's purebred. She cost four hundred dollars," said the little kid.

"Hoo," I replied, trying to sound like British royalty. I had to admit, though, that next to Astrid and Priscilla, Louie looked like a scruffy old orphan dog.

"Well," said the older girl. "I guess you should know that I'm Shannon Louisa Kilbourne. I live over there." She pointed to a house that was across the street, next door to the Papadakises. "And this is Amanda Delaney. She lives next door to me."

"But Priscilla and I have to go home now. So 'bye!" the little girl called gaily, and ran off.

"Well, I'm Kristy Thomas," I told Shannon. "You know where I live."

"In Mr. Brewer's house," she answered, clearly implying that I was not good enough to be a Brewer, just lucky enough to live with one. "Pew," she went on, "your dog smells. Where's he been? In a swamp?"

"Personally," I replied, ignoring her question, "I would rather live in a swamp than across the street from you."

"Oh, yeah? Well, you're only proving what

a jerk you are," retorted Shannon.

"And you're only proving what a snob you are."

"Jerk."

"Snob."

Shannon stuck her tongue out at me, I stuck mine out at her, and we walked on.

CHAPTER 4

Linny and Hannie Papadakis are neat little kids. They love to "play pretend" and to organize activities for the other neighborhood kids. And their little sister, Sari, is very sweet. All of the kids have dark hair, deep brown eyes, olive skin, and really terrific smiles.

On the afternoon that I was to baby-sit for them, Linny and Hannie were waiting for me in the front yard.

"Hi!" called Hannie, jumping up as soon as she saw me coming.

"Hi, you guys," I said.

"Guess what we want to do today," Linny said. "We want to have a pet fashion show."

"Yeah, we want to dress up Myrtle and Noodle," Hannie added.

This is the great thing about the Papadakises. They have just as much money as anyone else around here, but you wouldn't know it, except for the mansion. They're very down-

31

to-earth, and their pets are named Myrtle the Turtle and Noodle the Poodle, not Astrid of Grenville, like some pets I can think of. The children are allowed to choose their own clothes every morning, even though they sometimes end up wearing stripes with plaids, and they go barefoot all summer long.

"Let me talk to your mom first," I told Linnie and Hannie, "and then we'll see about Myrtle and Noodle."

"Okay," said Hannie cheerfully. She took my hand and led me inside the Papadakises' house. "Mo-om!" she yelled. "Kristy's here!"

Mrs. Papadakis came bustling through the hallway from the back of the house. "Hi, Kristy," she said. "Thanks for coming."

Linny, Hannie, and Sari look exactly like their mother. Mrs. Papadakis wears her dark hair so that it frames her face. And when she smiles her terrific smile, the corners of her wide-set brown eyes crinkle just the way Hannie's were crinkled then.

"I should be back by five o'clock," she told me. "I've got a meeting at the children's school."

"Okay," I replied. "Are there emergency numbers somewhere?" (As a baby-sitter, I always ask this if I'm working for a family I'm not too familiar with. You just never know what could happen.)

"Oh, yes," said Mrs. Papadakis. "I almost forgot. They're on the memo board in the kitchen. Pediatrician, grandparents, and George's — I mean, Mr. Papadakis' — office number."

"Great," I said. "Where's Sari?"

"Upstairs napping, but she should wake soon. And she'll want apple juice then. There's some in the refrigerator. But no snacks for the kids, okay?"

"Okay."

Mrs. Papadakis kissed Linny and Hannie and rushed off.

"Now," I said briskly, "what's this about dress — "

"WAHH!"

I was interrupted by a cry from upstairs.

"Oh, Sari's awake," said Linny.

"I'll get her," I told him. "Why don't you guys go play in the backyard?"

"Okay," they agreed.

"But stay there," I added. "Don't leave without telling me."

"Okay!" They were already halfway out the door.

I ran upstairs and followed the sound of

Sari's sobs to her bedroom. I opened the door slowly, knowing she would be confused to see me enter instead of her mother.

"Hi, Sari!" I said brightly.

The sobs increased.

I cheerfully pulled up the shade and straightened the room, talking to Sari all the time. "Hi, I'm Kristy," I told her. "We're going to have fun playing this afternoon."

"No, no, no, no, no!" wailed Sari.

But by the time I'd changed her, tickled her, and talked to her teddy bear, we were old friends. We walked down the stairs hand in hand. I gave her some apple juice, and then we joined Hannie and Linny in the yard.

"Hi, Sari-Sari!" cried Hannie, running over to her sister.

"Kristy," Linny said, "we want to have a fashion show for Myrtle and Noodle."

"You're going to dress up a turtle?" I replied. "Don't you think that's going to be kind of hard? Besides, where are you going to find turtle-size clothes?"

"Well, that's one of our problems," said Linny. "The other one is that we can't find Noodle. And we do have clothes for him. He fits into Sari's old baby clothes."

"Really?" I said.

"Yeah. For my pet show last summer, he

wore this little sundress and a bonnet and two pairs of socks."

I giggled. "Maybe Noodle was embarrassed and now he's hiding so you won't be able to do that to him again."

"Maybe . . ." said Linny doubtfully, not seeing anything funny about that.

My eyes drifted across the yard and over a low stone wall in search of Noodle. They landed in the yard next door — on one of the girls I had noticed at the bus stop. She looked like a short version of Shannon. She was sitting in the sun filing her nails and listening to a tape deck.

I nudged Linny. "Hey," I whispered, pointing to the girl. "Who's that?"

Linny looked across the yard. "That's Tiffany Kilbourne."

"Tiffany," I repeated. "She must be Shannon's sister."

"Yeah," said Linny. "She is. You know what? Sometimes Shannon baby-sits for us."

"She does?" I asked in surprise. "Do you like her?"

"Sure. She's neat."

"You know," I said, "I don't know too many people around here. Tell me who your neighbors are."

"Okay." Linny plopped to the ground, and

35

I joined him. Not far away, Hannie was playing "This Little Piggy" with Sari.

"Shannon and Tiffany have another sister, Maria. She's eight, like me. They all go to Stoneybrook Day School. But Hannie and I go to Stoneybrook Academy."

"Oh," I said. "Right. So does Karen. She and Hannie are in the same class."

"Yeah," agreed Linny with a smile. I could tell he was proud that I'd given him the responsibility of telling me about the neighborhood.

"Next door to the Kilbournes," he went on, pointing to the yard two houses away, "are the Delaneys. And they are — "

"Awful," Hannie supplied. She'd stopped wiggling Sari's toes and was listening to Linny and me.

"Really?" I asked. I'd met Amanda. She hadn't seemed too bad. "How are they awful?"

"Well, there are two of them," said Linny.

"Amanda and Max," Hannie added, making a horrible face.

"They're our ages." Linnie pointed to himself and Hannie. "Amanda's eight and Max is six."

"But we never, ever play with them," said Hannie. "Because they are mean and nasty and spoiled. And bossy. Mostly bossy."

"Wow," I exclaimed. I'd never heard Hannie get so worked up. I was about to ask them some more about the Delaneys when Shannon Kilbourne came out of her house and joined Tiffany in the yard. I know she'd seen me, but she pretended she hadn't. At first. After a few minutes, though, she began to stare at me.

How rude.

"Come on, you guys. Let's go inside," I said. "Maybe Noodle's there. We better find him."

Since Linny and Hannie are endlessly agreeable, they followed me into the house. I carried Sari on my hip.

"Noooo-dle!" Hannie called.

"Noooo-dle!" Linny called.

"Noooo-noo!" Sari called.

We hadn't gotten further than the living room when the phone rang. "I'll get it," I said. "You guys keep looking for Noodle."

I ran into the kitchen and picked up the phone. "Hello, Papadakis residence."

"Hello? Is that you, Kristy?"

The voice was vaguely familiar, but I couldn't quite place it. "Yes. This is Kristy. . . . Who's this?"

"It's Shannon Kilbourne next door. Listen, there's smoke coming out of the upstairs win-

37

dows at the Papadakises'. The house is on fire!"

I felt my stomach turn to ice. My knees buckled. This was the one thing I feared most when I was baby-sitting. A fire. But I had to stay calm. Don't panic, I told myself.

"Call the fire department!" I yelled at Shannon. Then I slammed down the phone and raced into the living room. I was hoping desperately that I would find all three kids together where I had left them.

But the only one there was Sari, sucking on one of her fingers. I scooped her up. From the other end of the house, I could hear Linny and Hannie calling for Noodle. I raced through the living room, a hallway, the library, and onto the sunporch. Thank goodness. There they were.

"Hannie, Linny," I said breathlessly, "I want you to pay very close attention to me. The house is on fire. We have to get out. There's no time to try to take stuff with us. Is there a way off the sunporch?"

"No," replied Linny. "It's not a real porch."

"We have to get Myrtle and Noodle!" Hannie cried, already sounding panicked.

"We can't," I told her, pushing her and Linny ahead of me into the library. "Now go straight to the front door. But don't run. You might fall."

The kids obeyed. On the way to the door, though, we passed Myrtle's box and in one swift movement, Linny stooped down, picked up the turtle, and kept on going. I didn't say anything.

As soon as we were out the front door, I cried, "Now you can run! Go right to the sidewalk, but don't run into the street."

Hannie and Linny ran, their legs pumping up and down. Myrtle was clutched between Linny's hands. Halfway across the lawn I dared to look back at the house. That's funny, I thought. I couldn't see even a wisp of smoke. I stopped. I sniffed the air. I didn't smell smoke, either. The house looked fine.

"Linny! Hannie! Stay where you are!" I called to them. They were standing on the sidewalk. Hannie was crying.

I was trying to decide whether it would be safe to approach the house with Sari in my arms, when I heard loud laughter from the Kilbournes' house. Shannon was in her front yard, doubled over. "Fake out! Fake out! Made you look!" she screeched.

I put Sari down and marched over to her. "Are you saying there's no fire?" I asked.

Shannon was laughing too hard to answer me.

So I stuck my tongue out at her and stomped away. I felt like a fool.

I calmed Hannie and Linny down, and then we found Noodle (who'd been napping under a bed). By then, Mrs. Papadakis was due home, so we never did hold the pet fashion show.

Of course, I had to tell Mrs. P. what had happened, since the false alarm was all Hannie and Linny could talk about. Mrs. P. became very angry, put her hands on her hips, and said, "I'll have to have a talk with Shannon before she sits again." But I didn't feel much better about the situation. All I wanted to do was get back at Shannon. The question was how?

The idea came to me early that evening, and I have absolutely no idea where it came from. One moment, I didn't know what to do about Shannon Louisa Kilbourne. The next moment, this great idea was in my head.

I got out a phone book, found the number of a diaper service, and dialed it.

"Mr. Stork's Diapers," said a pleasant-sounding man.

"Hello," I said. "I'm sorry to be calling so late, but this is sort of an emergency. My mom is sick, so we're going to need diaper service for my baby sister for about two weeks, starting tomorrow morning, if possible."

"Of course," replied the man. "Name please?"

"Shannon Kilbourne."

"Address?"

I gave the man the Kilbournes' address. When I went to bed that night, I was smiling.

And the next morning, I was delighted with what I saw from one of the guest bedrooms at the front of our house. It was the Mr. Stork truck. It pulled into the Kilbournes' driveway, and even from across the street I could hear bells jangling out "Rock-a-Bye, Baby." Then a man dressed as a stork dumped a huge package of diapers on the Kilbournes' front steps and drove off.

I was nearly hysterical.

Gotcha, Shannon! I thought.

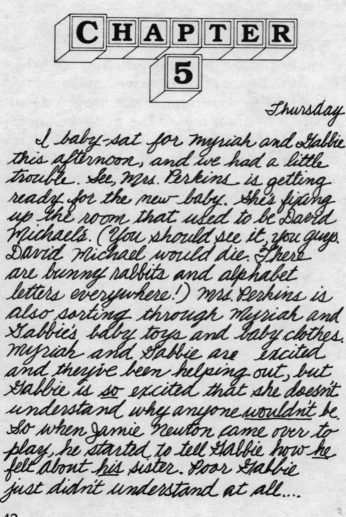

CHAPTER 5

Thursday

I baby-sat for Myriah and Gabbie this afternoon, and we had a little trouble. See, Mrs. Perkins is getting ready for the new baby. She's fixing up the room that used to be David Michael's. (You should see it, you guys. David Michael would die. There are bunny rabbits and alphabet letters everywhere!) Mrs. Perkins is also sorting through Myriah and Gabbie's baby toys and baby clothes. Myriah and Gabbie are excited and they've been helping out, but Gabbie is _so_ excited that she doesn't understand why anyone _wouldn't_ be. So when Jamie Newton came over to play, he started to tell Gabbie how _he_ felt about _his_ sister. Poor Gabbie just didn't understand at all....

42

Mary Anne loves to sit for the Perkinses now that she's gotten used to the fact that *they* live in *my* old house. Lucky for her such a nice family moved in. Even luckier that a new baby is on the way. Mary Anne is really excited. I know she's helped Mrs. Perkins paint the room and pick out curtain material — although the baby isn't due for several more months.

She's excited, and Myriah and Gabbie are, too. What the Perkins girls didn't realize was that not everybody would share their feelings.

As soon as Mrs. Perkins left on that Thursday, Jamie Newton came over to play. Myriah took him by the hand and said, "Come look at the baby's room. It is so, so beautiful. Mommy and Gabbie and I have been working very hard." She pulled Jamie up to the tiny room that used to belong to David Michael. Mary Anne and Gabbie followed.

"Oh, it looks great now!" Mary Anne exclaimed as they stood in the doorway. "You finished painting it."

"And one curtain is up, but Mommy's still hemming the other one."

"I didn't help my mommy with Lucy's room," said Jamie.

"How come?" asked Gabbie.

Jamie shrugged. "Just because."

"Well, we're helping," said Gabbie.

"You've been working hard," said Mary Anne, stepping inside the room.

"Look in the drawers," Myriah said to Mary Anne, "and you'll see what we did."

Mary Anne opened the drawers of the bureau to find piles of neatly folded sleepers and undershirts and jumpsuits.

"We washed everything that was in the box in the attic," Myriah told her. "And I folded all those clothes."

"Boy, I guess you're almost ready for this baby."

"Almost," agreed Myriah, "except for one important thing."

"What?" asked Mary Anne.

"We need a name for the baby. You want to hear the names Mommy and Daddy like? They like Sarah or Randi-with-an-'i' for a girl, or John Eric or Randy-with-a-'y' for a boy. But they haven't decided."

"What do you like?" I asked.

"I like Laurie for a girl, but I can't think of any good boys' names."

"I want to name it Beth," spoke up Gabbie.

"Laurie and Beth are both very pretty names," said Mary Anne. She glanced at Jamie. He was scowling.

"You know what I wanted to name my baby?

I wanted to name her Stupid-head."

"Stupid-head!" cried Gabbie. She looked crushed. "Nah-nah and a boo-boo. That is so, so mean."

"It is not," said Jamie. "I'm going home."

Gabbie marched out of the room. "I'm going to take a nap," she called crossly to Mary Anne.

"Wow," said Mary Anne to Myriah. "Gabbie sounds really mad."

"She must be upset about what Jamie said. We love our baby, even thought it isn't here yet."

"I'm glad you feel that way," said Mary Anne.

"How can Jamie be so mean?"

"I don't think he's being mean. He was jealous when Lucy was born. He used to be the baby of the family. Then everything changed for him. I think he felt a little scared."

"Now Gabbie feels bad," said Myriah.

"I know," agreed Mary Anne.

Myriah looked thoughtful. "Let's do something nice to make her feel better."

"That's a good idea," said Mary Anne. "Like what?"

"I'm not sure."

Myriah and Mary Anne sat down on the floor of the baby's room.

"What are some things Gabbie likes to do?" Mary Anne asked.

"She likes to color."

"What's something special that she can't do every day?"

"Go on rides at Disney World."

"Not that special. Something we could do this afternoon."

"I know!" said Myriah. "She likes tea parties. She likes to give tea parties for her dolls, but sometimes it's a big pain because she wants to get dressed up first, and dress her dolls and teddies, too."

"Well, let's have a tea party, then!" exclaimed Mary Anne. "I'll go downstairs and set it all up. We'll have juice and cookies. You and Gabbie get dressed up, and then dress up the dolls and animals. . . . I don't think Gabbie's really taking a nap, do you?"

"No way," replied Myriah.

So Mary Anne ran downstairs and found Gabbie's tea set in the playroom. She set eight places around the kitchen table. Then she put a cookie at every place, and filled the tiny teacups with Hawaiian Punch. She folded napkins and even grabbed a vase of flowers from the living room and put them in the middle of the table.

"Myriah! Gabbie!" she called from the bottom of the stairs. "Tea time!"

"We're not ready yet!" Myriah called back.

Mary Anne ran upstairs to see what was going on. In Gabbie's room she found Myriah wearing a pink party dress with white tights and shiny Mary Jane shoes. But Gabbie had had a different idea about getting dressed up. She was wearing one of her mother's slips, a necktie belonging to her father, a feather boa, a straw hat, sunglasses, and snow boots.

"How do I look?" she asked.

Mary Anne glanced at Myriah who shrugged.

"Lovely," Mary Anne told her.

"I'm all dressed up," she announced.

"I see. Are your dolls ready?" It was hard to tell. One of them was wearing sunglasses. Another was wearing a bathing cap.

"Yes," replied Gabbie, "but the bears aren't."

"Show us how to dress the bears," said Mary Anne. "Myriah and I will help you."

Gabbie instructed them to put undershirts and socks on the three bears, and then they carried the dolls and bears down to the kitchen, and sat them around the table.

"This is beautiful," said Gabbie, looking at the tea party and trying to sound grown up.

"It is too, too diveen," added Myriah.

Mary Anne giggled.

She and the girls drank their tiny cups of punch and ate their cookies. Then they drank the bears' and the dolls' punch and ate some of their cookies, too.

"Did you like the party?" Mary Anne asked Gabbie when it was over.

Gabbie nodded. "I loved it. It was too, too diveen."

Mary Anne smiled. The crisis was over.

CHAPTER 6

Linny and Hannie were right. The Delaney children are awful. They are nasty and bossy and everything Hannie said they are. I know because I baby-sat for them. Mrs. Delaney called the Baby-sitters Club, and of course my friends urged *me* to take the job since it's in my neighborhood.

I arrived at the Delaneys' after school on a Friday. (What a way to start the weekend.) Their house is the opposite of the Papadakises' or Watson's (I mean, mine). Last year, one of my spelling words was "ostentatious." (I'm a good speller.) And that's what the Delaneys' house was. Ostentatious. It was showy and show-offy and ornate. Guess what was in their front hall — a fountain. No kidding. There was this golden fish standing on its tail, fins spread, with water spouting out of its mouth and running into a little pool surrounding it.

Guess what's in our front hall — two chairs and a mirror.

Guess what's in the Papadakises' front hall — two chairs and Myrtle's box.

In the Delaneys' gigantic backyard are two tennis courts. In their library and living room are gilt-framed portraits and Oriental rugs, and the kitchen looks like a space control center with gadgets and buttons and appliances everywhere. I hope I never have to give the Delaney kids a meal. I wouldn't even be able to figure out how to toast a slice of bread. (I think the Delaneys' have a part-time cook, though.)

But I could have handled all this stuff okay. It was the children I couldn't take.

For starters, they weren't even interested in meeting me. Their mother answered the door, gave me instructions and phone numbers, and put on her coat, and still I hadn't seen the children.

"Where are Amanda and Max?" I finally asked.

"Oh, of course," said Mrs. Delaney, sort of breathlessly. "I suppose I ought to introduce you."

She led me into a room that I guessed was the family room, but it sure didn't look like ours. Our family room is always on the messy side — a newspaper strewn around, Louie lounging on the couch, Watson's cat, Boo-Boo, asleep on the television set, maybe a coloring book or some homework left out.

This room was not only tidy, it was clean. *And* it was all white. White shag rug, white leather couch, even white lacquer tables and a white TV set. Priscilla (fluffy and white, of course) sleeping daintily in a white wicker cat bed, looking as if somebody, maybe the director of a play, had posed her just so, to be the perfect complement to the perfect room.

Posed on the couch were two perfect (looking) children. Amanda, the eight-year-old I'd met with Shannon, her Mary Janes polished, her brown hair parted evenly and held in place with a big blue bow, sat primly on one side. She was wearing a blue corduroy jumper over a white blouse. Her jumper matched her hair ribbon exactly. Next to her was Max, the six-year-old, a blond-haired, blue-eyed angel of a boy, dressed in corduroy pants, an unwrinkled alligator shirt, and docksiders.

"Children," said Mrs. Delaney, "this is Kristy. She's going to baby-sit for you this afternoon. I'll be back in a couple of hours. You do what Kristy tells you, all right?"

Amanda and Max merely nodded, their eyes glued to the TV. Amanda didn't give any sign that she'd met me before.

Mrs. Delaney left then, and I sat down in a white armchair.

"Don't sit there!" Amanda squawked, and I leaped up.

"Why?" I asked.

"It's Daddy's chair."

This didn't make any sense to me, since Mr. Delaney wasn't at home, but I moved over to the couch anyway. Neither Max nor Amanda made any room for me, so I squished into a corner.

"What are you watching?" I asked the kids.

No answer.

But when a commercial came on, Amanda said, "Get me a Coke, Kristy."

"What do you say?" I replied in a singsong voice. When you have a little brother, a little stepbrother, and a little stepsister, you find yourself repeating this all the time, as a reminder to say "please" and "thank you."

"I say, 'Get me a Coke,' " Amanda repeated dryly.

"Get me one, too," said Max.

My mouth dropped open. What was I supposed to do? I couldn't very well scold Amanda and Max during the first fifteen minutes of my job. So I got up, went into the kitchen, found the Coke in the maze of appliances, and poured some into two glasses.

When I handed Amanda her glass, I didn't expect her to say "thank you" (I was too smart for that), but I also didn't expect her to say, "Where's the ice?"

I rolled my eyes, took the glasses back in the kitchen, dropped three ice cubes in each glass, and gave the Cokes to Amanda and Max. Amanda accepted hers and began to drink, but Max looked from me to his glass and back, and said, "I hate ice. Take it out."

Now if David Michael had said that to me, I would have replied, "Take it out yourself." But the Delaneys were new clients of the Baby-sitters Club, and I didn't want any unhappy children on hand when their mother returned. So I went to the kitchen for the third time and fished Max's ice cubes out of his glass with a spoon. When I handed the Coke back to him, he and Amanda drank in silence until their show was over.

"Well," I said, "let's go outside and play. There's nothing good on TV anyway."

Amanda shrugged. She handed me her empty glass and said, "Can you put this back in the kitchen? We're not allowed to leave stuff in here."

Max handed me his glass, too.

"And put them in the dishwasher," Amanda called after me.

I did so, my teeth clenched. Then I turned on a smile (a stiff one), walked back into the family room, and switched off the TV. "Time to go outside," I announced. "Come on."

Amanda and Max reluctantly followed me to the front door. So did Priscilla.

"Priscilla's a beautiful cat," I said to the kids, hoping, maybe, to start a conversation.

"She cost four hundred dollars," replied Amanda.

"I know. You told me." (Boy, what snobs.) "You know how much my dog Louie cost? Nothing. He was free."

"Oh, a mutt," said Max knowingly. "Too bad."

I rolled my eyes.

Then I opened the front door and who should I find there, hand poised to ring the bell, but David Michael. Louie was at his side.

"Hi!" I cried, unusually glad to see him. "What are you doing here?"

"Who's that?" interrupted Amanda before David Michael could answer.

"This is my brother, David Michael," I told her. "David Michael, this is Amanda Delaney and this is Max. Do you guys know each other?"

"I've seen them around," my brother said, just as Amanda said, "No."

The Snob kids and Priscilla and I joined David Michael and Louie outside. "What are you doing here?" I asked David Michael again.

"I just walked Louie over," he said.

"Is Louie your mutt?" asked Max.

"Louie is our *collie*," David Michael replied indignantly.

"He's not very pretty."

David Michael was completely taken aback.

"He's nothing like Priscilla," added Amanda. "Now *she* is beautiful. Look what good care she takes of her coat. Your dog — "

"Yeah?" David Michael challenged her, finally finding his voice.

"Well, he's just not pretty."

"Boys," David Michael informed her, "are not *supposed* to be pretty. Besides, he's old and he has arthritis."

"Ew," said Amanda. "I hope that never happens to Priscilla."

"David Michael, is anything wrong?" I asked him.

"I don't think Louie feels well," he said, his voice trembling.

"Well, Dr. Smith said he wouldn't. Remember?"

"I thought the pills were supposed to make him better."

"They're supposed to help take the pain away, but he still has arthritis," I pointed out.

At that moment, Louie lowered his head and sneezed loudly — *whoof!*

"Ew! Ew!" cried Amanda. "Disgusting. His sneeze got all over me! I'm going to wash my hands. You come with me, Kristy."

I looked at David Michael sympathetically. "I have to go inside. Why don't you take Louie home and let him rest? Maybe Mom could call Dr. Smith tomorrow."

"All right," David Michael agreed reluctantly. He turned and walked down the steps. "Come on, Louie," he urged. "Just three steps. You can do it." Louie followed him with his stiff-legged gait. As I looked after them, I sighed.

In the Snobs' opulent bathroom, Amanda commanded me to find first some violet-scented soap, and then a certain hand towel.

"Are you disinfected now?" I couldn't resist asking her when she was through washing her hands.

She gave me a dark look. "I don't know what that means. But at least your dog's germs are off me."

The phone rang then and Max said, "You get it, Kristy. It's in the kitchen."

(What? No phone in the bathroom?)

"Hello, Delaney residence," I said when I'd picked up the receiver. (Hello, Snob residence, I thought.)

"Kristy? Kristy? Is that you? This is Shannon."

My heart sank. She must have seen me when I crossed the Delaneys' yard. Had she figured out that I'd sent Mr. Stork to her?

"I'm baby-sitting at the Papadakises'," she said nervously. "I've been here dozens of times and nothing like this has ever happened."

"What's wrong?"

"Sari's crying and I can't get her to stop. She seems to like you, so I thought — "

"I'll be right over," I said, and hung up the phone. I wasn't sure I could trust Shannon, but I couldn't ignore a crying child. Sari could be sick or in pain. . . . "Amanda, Max, come on. We have to go to the Papadakises'. Now." Amid moans and groans, I rushed the kids out the door, across the Kilbournes' lawn, and to the Papadakises' front steps. I rang the bell and Shannon answered it. One of the bus stop girls (the brown-haired one) was with her.

"Yes?" said Shannon coolly.

"Here I am," I said, trying to catch my breath. "Where's Sari?"

"Why do you want to know?"

"I'm here to help — " I paused, listening. The house was silent. Shannon and her friend were trying not to laugh. I'd been tricked again.

At that moment, Hannie and Linny appeared. "Hi, Kr — " they started to say to me. Then they stopped, seeing Amanda and Max.

Amanda and Max immediately began whispering and giggling. Hannie and Linny frowned. Amanda pointed to her head, then to Linny, and said "Cuckoo" — just loudly enough for everyone to hear.

"I am not cuckoo," cried Linny. "*You* are!"

"Okay, okay," I said. I grabbed Amanda and Max by the hands, and headed for home. I was so mad, I couldn't even think of anything to say (or do) to Shannon.

The last thing I heard as we left the Papadakises' yard was Shannon yelling after me, "And thanks a lot for pushing me out of my baby-sitting jobs!"

Uh-oh, I thought.

CHAPTER 7

Saturday

I babysat for my brother tonight, and something is going on. Something's wrong. He hasn't been himself at all lately, but this was worse than usual. He was cross and mean and rude all evening. Finally we had this big fight and I couldn't believe what he said. I was so upset, I had to wait for Mom to come home so I could tell her about it. And then she called Dad in California to tell him about it.

This seems like personal, family business, but I guess you club members should know about it in case you sit for Jeff, because he's like a different kid these days. Better to be prepared. So this is what's going on . . . .

Wow. Talk about a different kid. Our even-tempered, unflappable alternate officer was a different person herself. Dawn was really upset. Not only did she write about Jeff in the club notebook, but she called both Mary Anne and me to tell us what had happened.

Apparently, ever since school began, Jeff has been having some problems. Actually, Dawn isn't sure if the problems are due to school starting again, or to the fact that Jeff got two letters on the first day of school, one from their father, one from Jeff's best friend in California. She thinks it's the letters' fault, though.

Dawn says Jeff has been acting up in class, and once he even walked right out in the middle of a reading lesson. He's had to stay after school twice, and go to the principal once. And he hasn't been too pleasant at home.

Anyway, Dawn's mom had needed a sitter on Saturday evening so she could go out with this guy Trip she's been seeing pretty often. Two of us were free that night, but of course we gave the job to Dawn since it was for her own brother.

The Trip-Man (that's what Dawn and Jeff call their mother's date) was going to pick Mrs. Schafer up at six-thirty. They were going to some fancy party in Stamford. Their evening was formal and would involve dinner, dancing, and entertainment. Dawn thought her mother looked very glamorous as she slipped on a long black gown with lots of sequins on the top part.

"You smell nice, too, Mom," Dawn told her mother as she hung around Mrs. Schafer's bedroom.

"It's my perfume, I guess. Want some?"

"No, thanks," said Dawn. "I like it better on you. You always smell like this when you go out. I like to smell the perfume and watch you get ready and dream about what you'll do on your date."

Mrs. Schafer smiled. "I used to do the same thing when *my* parents were getting ready to —"

"*You* were lucky enough to have *two* parents!" yelled Jeff from his bedroom.

Mrs. Schafer sighed. "He sounds like he's in another one of his moods," she said to Dawn.

"I heard that," Jeff shouted. "And it's not a mood!"

Dawn rolled her eyes. "You're making me take care of *that* all evening?" she teased.

"I'll give you a big tip," her mother replied. "Come on. Let's go downstairs and I'll show you what's for dinner."

Mrs. Schafer isn't much of a cook, but she

tries hard to make interesting health food for Dawn and Jeff. The Schafers are really into eating healthy, and are semi-vegetarians. They get tired of yogurt and salad and fruit, though, so Mrs. Schafer makes casseroles from vegetables and brown rice or pasta. She waits until she has a free day or weekend and then she makes four or five casseroles and freezes them.

Mrs. Schafer had just finished explaining to Dawn how to heat up an eggplant casserole when the doorbell rang. "That's Trip," she said. "You know where we'll be tonight. The number's on the fridge, and you can always call Granny and Pop-Pop if there's an emergency."

"I know," said Dawn. "Have fun, Mom. We'll be fine." She was pushing her mother toward the front door, all the while checking her over to make sure nothing was missing or out of place. (Mrs. Schafer is completely absentminded.)

"Good-bye, Jeff!" Mrs. Schafer called upstairs. "Have fun with Dawn."

" 'Bye," was the sullen reply.

Dawn and her mother shrugged. Then Mrs. Schafer answered the bell and Dawn said hello to the Trip-Man. Finally Dawn closed the door behind her mom, and breathed a sigh of relief.

She began to get dinner ready. She set the table, put out whole-wheat rolls, and poured glasses of iced herbal tea. All the while, she knew she should be asking Jeff to help her (even if she *was* the baby-sitter), but it seemed better to leave him alone when he was in one of his moods.

When the casserole was ready, Dawn called Jeff to supper. He walked into the Schafers' old-fashioned kitchen, saw the table, and said, "It's Saturday. And Mom's not here. Why aren't we eating in front of the TV?"

"Because we'll turn into couch potatoes, that's why," said Dawn, trying to be funny.

Jeff grumbled some answer that Dawn couldn't understand, filled his plate, then began to carry it into the family room. "I want to watch *Leave It to Beaver*, not sit in here," he said over his shoulder.

"Then put your dinner on a tray," Dawn told him. "Otherwise you'll spill." She took two trays out of a cabinet, but before she could hand one to him, he shrugged away, saying, "And I *won't spill*. I don't need a tray. *I am not a baby.*"

"Well, I'm using one, and I'm older than you are," Dawn retorted. She couldn't help sounding just a little cross.

Jeff ignored her and settled himself in the

family room, watching *Leave It to Beaver*. He balanced his plate on his knees and his glass on the arm of the couch. Dawn sat beside him.

Sure enough, about halfway through the program, Jeff knocked over his tea. As he dove to catch the glass before it hit the floor, the food slid off his plate, into his lap, and all over the couch.

"Oh, Jeff!" exclaimed Dawn, quickly setting her tray on the coffee table and getting to her feet.

Before she could say another word, Jeff was on his feet, too. "Don't say anything!" he yelled. "This wasn't my fault!"

"Oh, no? Well, whose fault was it?"

"You and Mom always treat me like a baby! I am not a baby! I'm in fifth grade!"

"Jeff," Dawn said, "you're the one who just knocked over his entire dinner."

Now maybe this wasn't the most tactful thing Dawn could have said, but it was true.

"If you'd treat me like a grown-up person I'd act like a grown-up person!" Jeff's voice rose. He was yelling. Not just talking loudly, but really shouting. "I don't need a baby-sitter! I'm too old for one. Mom treats me like a baby. You treat me like a baby. The only one who doesn't treat me like a baby is Dad."

"Whoa," said Dawn under her breath. Personally, she didn't think she and her mother babied Jeff at all. He was ten, the same age as the Pike triplets, whom the club members sit for all the time. In fact, Jeff was often on his own during the day, something Mrs. Pike rarely allows for the triplets.

"Jeff," Dawn began. He was facing her angrily while tea seeped into the couch and eggplant casserole dripped down the front of his jeans.

"Shut up!" cried Jeff. "Just shut up! I hate it here. I miss California. I *hate* living with you and Mom! I wish I lived with Dad."

Jeff left the mess on the couch, ran upstairs, and locked himself in his room. Dawn decided it would be better to leave him alone. Slowly, she cleaned up the couch. Then she tried to finish her own dinner, but it was cold, so she cleaned up the kitchen instead.

Dawn told Mary Anne she felt stunned. (She called Mary Anne that evening while she was waiting for her mother to come home.) She said Jeff might as well have hit her. That was how bad she felt. Mary Anne isn't allowed to talk on the phone for more than ten minutes at a time, so Dawn had to hang up much sooner than she wanted. Then she called me.

She was really scared for Jeff. She'd seen him get angry plenty of times, but she'd *never* seen him act like this.

Mrs. Schafer had said she'd probably be home around twelve-thirty or one o'clock. Dawn knew she had to wait up for her, but one o'clock seemed like centuries away, and Dawn was a nervous wreck. She tried to keep busy. She read a short ghost story, but when she was done, realized she hadn't paid a bit of attention and would have to read it again sometime. Finally, she just parked herself in front of the TV and watched one show after another until the Trip-Man brought her mother home.

As soon as Dawn heard the car in the driveway, she ran to the front hall and blinked the outside lights as a signal to her mother. Then she flung open the front door. Mrs. Schafer was already halfway up the walk.

"Mom! Mom!" called Dawn.

"Honey, what on earth is wrong? Are you and Jeff all right?"

"I am, but Jeff isn't," Dawn replied as her mother stepped into the house.

Dawn told Mrs. Schafer everything that had happened. "He said he wants to go back to California, Mom," she finished up. "And he sounds like he means it."

Mrs. Schafer had turned slightly pale. "Oh,

boy," she said. "Maybe that trip to California this summer wasn't a good idea. It must have made him homesick."

"Well, it made *me* homesick," Dawn admitted, "but I still wanted to come back to Connecticut — and you."

"Thanks, honey," said her mother, giving Dawn a little hug. "I guess you and Jeff are just different. Everybody always says a boy needs his father. I thought that was very old-fashioned, but maybe it's true."

"Mom, you're not going to send Jeff back to Dad, are you?" Dawn was horrified. "We wouldn't be a family then. We'd be split in half."

"Oh, Dawn. We'll always be a family. But don't worry. I couldn't just send Jeff back to your father, even if I wanted to. At least not right away. I have custody of him. Legal custody. But I do think I better talk to your father. And," Mrs. Schafer added, "you better go to bed. It's one-thirty. You'll be a zombie tomorrow."

Dawn went to bed reluctantly. She noticed that Jeff's light was out and wondered when he'd gone to bed. She hadn't seen him since he'd run upstairs during dinner.

In the next room, Mrs. Schafer phoned Dawn's father. It was only ten-thirty in California. Not too late. Dawn pressed her ear against the wall and tried to overhear her mother's end of the conversation, but the words were muffled. She could tell that her mother was upset, though. Dawn sighed. Her family was just getting used to being divorced. She'd thought the bad times were over. Now, she wasn't so sure.

CHAPTER 8

"Come to order," I said listlessly. I said it so listlessly that nobody heard me and I had to repeat myself. It was pathetic. I tapped a pencil on the edge of Claudia's desk and wished I had a gavel.

It was a gloomy day, gloomy outside and gloomy inside. Nobody felt like having a meeting of the Baby-sitters Club. Dawn and I were depressed. Claudia was mad because she'd flunked a spelling test. Mary Anne was upset because her kitten, Tigger, had worms. And Stacey was upset because she had a doctor's appointment coming up and she hates doctor's appointments.

"We're *in* order," said Mary Anne. "Sort of."

"Any club business?" I asked.

My friends shook their heads.

"Boy, what a lousy, stinky, rotten day," I commented.

"Yeah," agreed the others.

"Have I told you about the Snob family?" I asked. "Amanda and Max?"

"You mean the Delaneys?" said Mary Anne, frowning down at the client list in our record book.

"I mean the Snobs," I said pointedly. "You guys, those kids are terrors. They make Jenny Prezzioso look like Little Miss Muffet."

"You're kidding. What'd they do?" asked Claudia. (Claudia once unexpectedly sat for some terrors herself — Jamie Newton's cousins — and she hasn't gotten over the experience. Stories about other terrors are always of special interest to her.)

"They are spoiled rotten," I told her. "They're demanding, they're rude, and they're snobby. We're watching TV, right? And at the commercial Amanda says to me, 'Get me a Coke.' Just like that. 'Get me a Coke.' No please or anything. And so I say, 'What do you say?' You know, like I always say to David Michael and Karen and Andrew. And she gives me this look and says, 'I say, "Get me a Coke."' Can you believe her nerve? Then *Max* says, 'Get me one, too.' So I do, but Amanda says, 'Where's the ice?' and I get ice and then Max doesn't want it. Then later they order me to put the empty glasses in the dishwasher and

70

to answer the phone. Which I would have done anyway. But you don't expect an eight-year-old and a six-year-old to order you around."

"Why did you let them?" asked Stacey.

"Because . . . I don't know. I mean, what would you have done? They're new clients. We have to be nice to them. We don't want Mrs. Snob coming home and hearing the little Snobs saying, 'Oh, that Kristy is so mean. She makes us say please and thank you and get our own Cokes.' Besides, I can't force them to do anything they don't want to do."

Stacey laughed. "No, but there are ways to get around those kids. Believe me. You don't have to — "

Ring, ring.

Stacey interrupted herself to answer the phone. "Hello, Baby-sitters Club. . . . Oh, hi, Mrs. Delaney."

"Mrs. *Delaney?*" I whispered. I made a gagging sound and pretended to choke. Stacey turned away so she wouldn't have to look at me.

"Next Tuesday?" she was saying. "Both kids. Okay. . . . Okay. . . . I'll call you right back." She hung up the phone and turned around. "Kristy, don't *do* that!" she exclaimed, giggling. "You almost made me laugh. And I almost called Mrs. Delaney 'Mrs. Snob'!"

We all laughed then and felt a little better. Claudia, the junk-food addict, found a bag of Gummi Bears stashed inside her pillow case and passed them around to those of us who'll eat candy (herself, Mary Anne, and me). Then she found some M&M's and passed those around, too.

Mary Anne was looking at our appointment calendar. "Three of us are free on Tuesday," she reported.

I wrinkled up my nose. *I* certainly didn't want to sit for the Delaneys again.

"It's you, Stacey, and Dawn," Mary Anne went on.

I noticed that Dawn looked as unenthusiastic as I felt.

"Can I go?" asked Stacey.

"*Can* you?!" I replied. "Be my guest. You can be the Delaneys' permanent baby-sitter, for all I care."

"Great," replied Stacey. "Because I know just how to handle the Snobs."

Once again she was interrupted by the ringing phone. We took a couple of jobs then and called Mrs. Delaney back, and when we were done, we'd forgotten all about Stacey's plans, whatever they were.

"You know," I said, leaning back in the director's chair and yawning, "there might be another snob-related problem. Not with *the* Snobs, but with the snobby girls I told you about. Shannon and Tiffany and their friends."

"Is Shannon the one who was mean to Louie?" asked Mary Anne, who has a soft spot in her heart for animals.

"Yes," I replied. "And the thing is, I didn't know it at first, but I guess she baby-sits in the neighborhood, too. I know she sits for the Papadakises anyway. And the other day she accused me of pushing her out of her sitting jobs."

"Oops," said Claudia.

"Right," I replied.

"Well, she can't be the only baby-sitter in the neighborhood," Dawn countered. "I mean, look at us. You started this club so there would be enough sitters to go around."

"That's true," I said slowly.

We were sitting silently, the five of us mulling this problem over, when all of a sudden Dawn began to cry. The rest of us looked at each other with our eyebrows raised. Not only is Dawn not a crier, but, well, what was she crying about?

"Dawn?" Mary Anne ventured. She and Dawn were sitting on Claudia's bed, and Mary Anne scrunched over until she was right next to her. "Dawn, what's the matter?" she asked worriedly.

At first Dawn just shook her head. She couldn't talk. Then she opened the club notebook and pointed to the account she'd written of sitting for her brother.

"Oh, you're upset about Jeff?" asked Mary Anne.

Dawn nodded, sniffling.

Mary Anne and I filled Claudia and Stacey in on the news, in case they hadn't gotten around to reading the notebook. Then, when Dawn had control of her voice, she added that her mother had had a long talk with her father, and that her father, for some reason, hadn't seemed crazy about the possibility of Jeff's living with him.

"I don't know," Dawn said, (only, with her stuffed nose, it sounded like "I dote dough"). "I don't know which is worse, the thought that Jeff hates living with Mom and me and wants to leave us, or the thought that maybe Dad doesn't want him. And," she went on, "if Dad doesn't want *him*, I assume he wouldn't want *me*, either. Not that I'd like to move back to California. It's just that it's awful to think your father doesn't want you."

"Tell me about it," I said bitterly. My parents' divorce hadn't exactly been friendly, and my dad never writes or calls my brothers and me. I don't think he cares about us at all. "But Dawn, are you *sure* he doesn't want you and Jeff?" I asked. "Maybe he's just enjoying being a bachelor again. I mean, first he was a family man, then he probably got used to living with*out* you and Jeff and your mom, and now he's just, I don't know, unsettled by the thought of *another* change."

"You know," said Dawn, brightening, "maybe you're right. I mean, he didn't say, 'I don't want Jeff.' He said something about having to change his work hours, and needing to get a housekeeper. Stuff like that."

We all agreed that Mr. Schafer was probably an okay dad who'd just been taken by surprise by the ten-thirty phone call. The meeting ended then, and I went home feeling subdued. I had problems, we all had problems. At the moment, Dawn's were the biggest. (They were certainly bigger than Tigger's worms.) Although I knew our problems would work out eventually, I realized that, as a group, we were kind of under the weather.

Charlie parked the car in the garage and we went inside. We found Watson home early, starting dinner. In the living room, Sam was helping David Michael with a tricky subtraction problem. Boo-Boo watched them from an armchair. Maybe because he's a cat, or maybe just because he's Boo-Boo, he always seems to watch people suspiciously, as if, right now, my brothers weren't doing math, they were plotting ways to torture Boo-Boo.

"Louie!" I called. "Louie! Where are you, boy?"

"Woof!"

Louie's woof came from Watson's library. I wandered in that direction and found him curled up on an Oriental rug.

"Hey, David Michael!" I yelled. "Did you feed Louie?"

"I put his food out and called him to dinner but he wouldn't come," he replied.

"Okay!" I knelt next to Louie. "Don't you want supper?" I asked him.

Louie's head was resting on one of his front paws. In order to look at me, he raised his eyes, but he didn't move his head.

"Come on, it's supper time," I told him, trying to sound excited about it. "Time for doggie treats. Maybe David Michael will let you have a people cracker later. Remember how much you liked the one in the shape of the vet?"

"Mmm-mm," whimpered Louie.

"Come on, I know you're hungry. All you have to do is stand up and walk into the kitchen. . . . Come *on*."

I stood up, urging Louie to get up, too. He staggered to his feet — and I mean *staggered*. He got his front legs up first and tried to raise his hindquarters, but his left front paw collapsed and he fell stiffly. Finally I picked him up around his middle and held him in place until all four legs were steady. Louie and I started toward the kitchen. But we hadn't even left the library when Louie jerked to a stop, squatted, and had an accident on one of Watson's Oriental carpets.

"Louie!" I scolded. "Mo-om! . . . Watson, is Mom home yet?"

"Kristy, what's wrong?" called Sam. He and David Michael came running.

"What's wrong? *That* is what's wrong." Louie was getting painfully to his feet, and I pointed to the mess on the carpet.

"Louie!" David Michael cried. "How could you do that? He's never done that," he said to Sam and me. "Never."

"Oh, he did it all the time when he was a puppy," replied Sam mildly. "I'll go get some paper towels."

Louie knew he'd done something wrong and he slunk out of the library with his tail between his legs.

"Bad, bad dog!" exclaimed David Michael, shaking his finger at Louie. "You're not a puppy now." But then he bent down to hug him. "Louie, I'm sorry," he said. "I didn't mean that. I don't think you could help yourself. Could he, Kristy?"

I shook my head. "No, he couldn't."

David Michael looked at me from around Louie's furry neck. "He's really sick, isn't he?" he asked.

I nodded. Then I turned away before my brother could see me cry.

CHAPTER 9

Tuesday

Okay, so I sat for the snobs today, and no big deal. You just have to know how to handle them. You have to know a little psychology. And I happen to. Know psychology, that is. I read this magazine article called "Getting What You Want: Dealing With Difficult People the Easy Way." It's kind of hard to explain what you're supposed to do, so I'll just give you some examples of how I dealt with the snobs. And you'll see that they can be tamed. Plus, I found that once you have tamed them, they're pretty nice little kids.

By the way, my parents have a book called <u>The Taming of the Shrew</u>. I think it might be a play. Now I could write a play called <u>The Taming of the Snobs</u>!...

Well, we were all pretty impressed with Stacey and her psychology. Especially since her job at the Snobs' started out as badly as mine had, maybe even worse. This time, when Mrs. McGill had dropped Stacey off at the Delaneys', Mrs. Delaney took Stacey upstairs to the little Snobs' playroom. Amanda and Max, looking gorgeous and immaculate, of course, were standing in the middle of the messiest room Stacey had ever seen. It was even messier than the way the Barretts' house used to look when Dawn first began baby-sitting for the impossible three. There were toys everywhere, and not just big toys, but Tinker Toys, Matchbox cars, and Legos, all mixed in with stuffed animals, board games, dolls, dress-up clothes, you name it. It was toy soup. And Mrs. Delaney asked Stacey, Amanda, and Max to clean it up before they did anything else.

"Well," said Stacey when Mrs. Delaney had left, "let's get this room in shape. Then we can go outside."

"If you want to go outside, then clean it yourself," said Amanda. "We like it messy." She stood back, folded her arms, and glared at Stacey. Max imitated her.

Stacey was prepared for something like this. She pretended to gaze around the room. Then she said seriously, "You know, you're right. I like a really messy room. In fact, I don't think this room is messy enough. Look at this. A whole set of Lincoln Logs. They're not even on the floor." Stacey poured the Lincoln Logs into the toy soup.

"Hey!" cried Amanda. "What do you think you're doing?"

"Yeah! What are you doing?" added Max.

"You said you like a messy room," Stacey replied. "Well, I do, too." She picked up a stack of construction paper and let it start floating to the floor, piece by piece.

"Quit messing up our room!" shouted Amanda. She held her arms stiffly at her sides and stamped her foot.

"Why?" demanded Stacey, pausing long enough to let the remainder of the paper settle into the toy soup. Then she began scattering puzzle pieces.

"Because," said Max. "That's why."

"I thought you liked a good mess," Stacey went on.

"We do," Amanda began, then hesitated. "But not . . . not this good a mess. Cut it out!"

"I'm just trying to help you guys out," Stacey told her.

"No! I mean . . . we want it clean." Amanda scrambled around, picking up the paper.

"Whoops! You forgot these doll clothes," said Stacey. She dumped out a box of Barbie dresses. Max grabbed them up and shoved them back in the box. "CUT IT OUT!" he screeched.

Before Stacey knew it, the Snobs were cleaning up the room. After a while, Stacey pitched in, but neither Amanda nor Max said a word about it. They just kept glancing at her warily.

When the room was as neat as a pin, the Snobs stood in the doorway to admire their work. Stacey thought they looked pretty proud of themselves, but she knew better than to praise them. After all, they'd been tricked, and they probably knew it.

"Boy, am I thirsty," said Max. "Get me some milk, Stacey."

"Milk?" repeated Stacey. "Okay. And I guess while I'm at it, I'll get some orange juice, some Hawaiian Punch, maybe some iced tea — "

"No, no," Max interrupted her. "Um, that's okay. I'll just get it myself."

"Yeah, we'll get the milk ourselves," added Amanda.

"I'll join you," said Stacey, and followed them downstairs.

Max got a carton of milk out of the Snobs' space-age refrigerator. Stacey watched Amanda take two glasses out of a cabinet, think better of it, and remove a third for Stacey.

Then Max held the carton out to Stacey. "Pour," he commanded, and Stacey knew he was testing her.

"Okay," said Stacey. But instead of taking the milk carton from Max, she opened a cupboard and began removing glasses and setting them on the table.

"*Now* what are you doing?" asked Amanda.

"Well, Max just said, 'pour.' He didn't say how much he wanted. I thought I'd better be prepared."

"Oh, never mind." Amanda took the carton crossly from Max and filled two glasses with milk. She hesitated. Then, "Do you want some?" she asked Stacey.

"Yes, please. Half a glass will be fine."

Amanda poured half a glass for Stacey and pushed it across the table to her. The three of them sat down and drank in silence. It wasn't long before Max knocked into his glass, sloshing milk over the sides.

He stared at the puddle on the table. "Wipe it up, Stacey," he commanded.

"Could you finish spilling it first, please?"

"Huh?" said Amanda and Max at the same time.

"Finish spilling it first. You've only spilled some of it. I don't want to have to stand up and get the sponge now if I'm just going to have to get it again in a few minutes. And by the way, since you like me to clean things up for you so much, you ought to know that I'll be happy to give you a bath later, I'm sure you'll want me to clean *you* up, as well as everything else."

"That just shows how much you know," said Max, pouting. "I don't want you to give me a bath. I don't want you to clean up *any*thing for me. I'll clean up my own messes. So there."

"Suit yourself," Stacey replied as Max mopped up the spill.

Max not only wiped up the mess, he brushed a few crumbs from the table, carried the sponge and the crumbs back to the sink, dropped the crumbs down the drain, and rinsed the sponge out before returning to the table.

"Thank you," said Stacey.

"You're welcome," replied Max.

"Stacey? What would happen if I asked you to get us some cookies?" ventured Amanda.

"Well, if you said, 'Stacey, could you please get out the Oreo cookies,' I would probably do it, especially if I thought you were going to thank me when I put them on the table. But if you just said, 'Stacey, get us the cookies,' then I would give you every kind of cookie I could find, because I wouldn't be sure what you meant, and I wouldn't want to have to jump up and get anything *else* for a person who never says please or thank you."

Amanda nodded thoughtfully.

"Aside from which," added Stacey, "I would feel very, very sorry that you are eight years old and unable to get cookies yourself."

Amanda nodded again. Stacey thought she saw Max hide a smile. Then he said, "*I* can clean up myself."

"I know," replied Stacey. "I'm glad to see that." She smiled at Max, then turned to Amanda. "*Do* you want some cookies?"

"No," said Amanda. "I just wanted to find out what would happen if I asked for them."

Stacey certainly hadn't expected *that* from the Snobs, but Amanda didn't seem to be acting snide or rude. In fact, she looked quite serious.

"You know," said Stacey, "you guys have worked really hard this afternoon. I think we should do something fun for now."

"Like what?" asked Amanda.

"Do you know how to play hopscotch?" asked Stacey.

"Hopscotch is boring," said Amanda.

"It's for *girls*," added Max witheringly.

"Would you relax? I just asked if you knew how to play. I didn't ask if you wanted to play. Now. *Do* you know how to play hopscotch?"

"Yes."

"Yes."

"Do you have any chalk?"

"Yes."

"Yes."

"Do your parents let you draw on the driveway with chalk?"

"Yes."

"Yes."

"Good," said Stacey. "Because I'm going to teach you how to play Snail, and it helps to know how to play hopscotch first."

"Snail?" replied Amanda, intrigued. "What's that?"

"It's a very cool game," Stacey replied, "and I guarantee that if you show it to your friends, they will all want to play Snail with you. Now let's put our glasses in the dishwasher and go."

Without so much as a complaint, Amanda and Max marched their glasses to the sink, rinsed them out, and put them in the dishwasher. Stacey did the same with her glass.

Then Max found a box of chalk and he and Stacey and Amanda went outdoors to the driveway where they found Priscilla sitting primly in a patch of shade.

Priscilla and the Snobs watched as Stacey drew a gigantic spiral on the driveway. Then she blocked the spiral off in boxes about a foot long, like this:

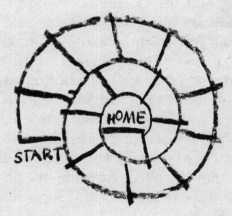

"Okay," said Stacey, "the object of Snail is to hop from the outside to the center of the snail shell, one foot in each square. If you make it all the way to Home without stepping on any lines, you get to choose one square for yourself. You write your initial on it. Later, when you hop to one of your own squares, you can land in it with two feet and rest there. But everyone else has to jump *over* it. When so many squares are taken that we can't play anymore, the person with the most squares is the winner. Understand?"

The Snobs nodded. They were actually smiling. They even let Stacey go first so she could demonstrate.

Stacey and the Delaneys played Snail until Mrs. Delaney came home. Stacey said she actually had fun — and she thinks Amanda and Max did, too. They giggled and shrieked, groaned when they missed, cheered when they earned new squares. The only sign of the old Delaneys was when Amanda ordered Stacey to get her a piece of chalk. "Maybe I better take your next turn for you, too," said Stacey.

"No, no," replied Amanda hastily, but a giggle threatened to escape. "Sorry. I'll get the chalk myself."

The game continued.

Mrs. Snob paid Stacey very well for the afternoon. She was especially pleased to see the tidy playroom. When the Delaneys dropped Stacey off at her house, she called good-bye to Amanda and Max, who answered cheerfully, but as the door was closing behind her,

Stacey heard Amanda say, "Mom, no kidding, she was the *weirdest* baby-sitter we've ever had."

Apparently, Mrs. Snob didn't mind. She called the Baby-sitters Club again very soon.

And I got the job.

CHAPTER 10

I read Stacey's entry in our club diary, and while I had to admit that she'd certainly handled the Snobs well, I also had to admit that I didn't *quite* understand what her method had been.

"I don't get it," I said to Stacey at lunch one day. "What were you doing? Just weirding them out by giving them unexpected answers?"

"Not exactly," replied Stacey. "I started out by going along with everything they said — but taking an extra step. Like when Amanda told me she liked a messy playroom, I not only agreed with her, I added to the mess."

"I wonder why that made her clean it up?" I said slowly.

"Well, actually," Stacey answered, "I think two things were going on then. First of all, the Snobs like to be contrary, which I was counting on — that was the psychology part —

but second, I think I did sort of weird them out. I was like Mary Poppins gone crazy, and they just wanted some normalcy. So cleaning up the playroom seemed a lot more normal than letting me do what I was doing."

I nodded.

"But later," said Stacey, "something else happened which I hadn't planned on at all. I realized that Max thought I was accusing him of being a baby. You know, by hinting that he wasn't able to mop up his spill or do other things by himself. Then I used that against both him and Amanda and it seemed pretty effective. No kid likes to think that anyone else thinks he or she is a baby."

"Pretty smart, Stace," I said. "I hope I can remember all this tomorrow."

I was going to sit at the Snobs' the next day, and I intended to be prepared for anything and anyone — fires, emergencies, Shannon, and especially the Snobs' behavior.

As I crossed the street to the Delaneys' the next afternoon, I kept repeating to myself, "Go along with everything they say, and take it one step further." It sounded easy enough, but I knew I'd have to think quickly.

Mrs. Delaney left as soon as I arrived, and I found myself facing the Snobs again. Well, not exactly facing them, since Amanda was up in her room and Max was out in the garage, but you know what I mean.

Amanda was in her room because she had been assigned to re-work some math problems that her teacher thought she could do a better job on. As soon as she saw me in her doorway, she said, "Kristy, come here. Do this problem for me. I hate fractions."

"Sure," I replied, "It's unfortunate that I'm so bad at fractions, though. I mean, I like them and everything, but I always make mistakes. Oh, well. Here. Give me your book." I held out my hand.

"That's okay," said Amanda, hugging her math book to her chest. "I'll do it myself. No problem."

"No problem!" I cried. "Hey, that's a pretty good pun. *Problem?* As in math problem? Get it?"

Amanda managed a smile.

"Come downstairs when you're finished," I told her. "Maybe we could play Snail. Stacey taught me the game, and she said she taught you, too."

I went to the garage to see what Max was up to. I found him swinging back and forth on a rope that had been tied to a beam in the eaves. He was singing, "Oh, I've never, never,

never in my long-legged life seen a long-legged sailor with his long-legged wife!"

I giggled. "Where'd you learn that song?" I asked him. "It's funny."

"Our music teacher taught it to us today," he replied, slowing down. "He taught us another song, too. About a cat. But I don't understand something. What kind of cat is a hysle cat?"

I frowned. "I don't know. Why don't you sing me the song? Maybe we can figure it out."

Max sang three verses of the song. Each time he came to the chorus, he would sing, "My hysle cat, my hysle cat," and touch his head the way his music teacher had shown the class.

In the middle of the fourth verse, I began to laugh. "Max!" I exclaimed. "This isn't a song about a cat. It's a song about a hat. Try saying, 'My high silk hat' instead of, 'My hysle cat.' "

"What? . . . Oh!" Suddenly Max understood. He began to laugh, too. Then he jumped off the swing and ran around the garage singing, "My hysle cat! My high silk hat!"

"What are you guys doing?" a voice demanded.

Amanda was standing in the doorway to the garage.

"Oh, sorry," I said. "Are we being too loud?"

"No," replied Amanda crossly. "I'm done with my homework. Now Max and I want a snack. Right, Max?"

"Right," he replied, even though I'm sure he had been thinking about hats and cats, not snacks, before his sister showed up.

"Fix us a snack, Kristy," Amanda demanded.

"Okay," I said. "But from your tone of voice, I can tell you're very hungry, so I think I'll fix you dinner instead. Your mom won't mind if I use the kitchen, will she? Now let's see," I rushed on. "My specialties are monkeys' liver, braised goat's tongue, and rabbit brains. You know Mrs. Porter across the street?"

"Morbidda Destiny?" whispered Max. (My stepsister, Karen, has all the kids around here thinking that lonely old Mrs. Porter is a witch whose real name is Morbidda Destiny.)

"Right. I get all my herbs and spices from her," I told the Snobs.

Both Max and Amanda were staring at me incredulously. Suddenly Amanda's face broke into a smile. "That's a joke, right?" she said.

"Yeah," I agreed. "It's a joke."

"You're funny," Amanda said. "Come on. Let's play Snail."

"I thought you wanted a snack."

"Nah. We already had one."

"Monkey's liver!" cried Max, giggling. "Hey, did you ever hear that gross song? It goes, 'Great big globs of greasy, grimy — ' "

"Max!" Amanda shrieked. "Don't sing that! It makes me sick. . . . I'll race you to the chalk."

Amanda and Max and I were halfway through our game of Snail, and the Snobs had run indoors for drinks of water, when a white van drove up the Delaneys' driveway. Large red letters on the sides spelled PIZZA EXPRESS. The driver jumped out and approached me with a flat white box.

"You Kristy Thomas?" he asked. "Here's your pizza."

"My pizza?"

"Yeah. You and your friend called about half an hour ago. The gigglers?"

It took a second for this to sink in. Then, in a flash, I realized what had happened. "Oh," I said, with a little laugh. "You want Kristy *Thomas*. Right. Well, I'm — I'm just the babysitter. Genevieve. Kristy is next door. With her, um, giggly friend. You'll recognize her right away. She's got long, wavy blonde hair. She wants the pizza over there. Really," I added when the deliveryman looked at me skeptically.

"You're sure about this?" he said as he climbed back into the truck.

"Positive," I replied, glad the Snobs hadn't heard me telling lies.

I watched the truck back down the driveway, turn into the street, and head for the Kilbournes'. I ran to the front of the Delaneys' house for a better view, and hid behind a shrub just in time to see Shannon and Tiffany answer their door, argue with the poor pizza guy, and then crossly shove some money into his hand as he gave them the pizza.

The next thing I knew, Shannon and Tiffany were marching angrily over to the Delaneys', followed by Astrid of Grenville.

"Uh-oh," I said. I dashed around the corner of the house and into the garage, where I bumped into Amanda and Max. "Indoors," I hissed, and pushed them inside before they could say a word. As soon as the door was shut behind us, we heard a *ding-dong*.

"I'll get it!" cried Max.

"No, don't — " I started to say, but it was too late.

Max was racing to the front door. He threw it open. Shannon, Tiffany, and Astrid were standing on the Delaneys' steps. Shannon was holding a wobbly PIZZA EXPRESS box. Grease stains were appearing on the sides.

"You owe me money," was the first thing Shannon said.

"Who, me?" I asked innocently.

"Yes, you. The deliveryman said someone named *Genevieve* sent him over to our house with a pizza for Kristy Thomas, and then he described *me*."

"So why do I owe you money?" I asked. "My name isn't Genevieve."

"Why?" Shannon spluttered. "You know very well why. You told him *your* name was Genevieve and *my* name was . . ."

"But you started this whole thing. *You* ordered the pizza. *I* just outsmarted you," I said maddeningly.

Shannon narrowed her eyes. *"You* horned in on my baby-sitting territory. My sister and I used to be the only sitters around here." She opened the box and began to ease a gooey slice away from the rest of the pie. "How'd you like pizza in your face?"

"No! Don't throw it!" shrieked Amanda. "Mommy and Daddy just had the hall painted. And the fish fountain cost two thousand dollars!"

Shannon hesitated long enough for me to say, "You throw that at me and I'll throw it back at Astrid. You'll have a pepperoni mountain dog."

Shannon dropped the slice back into the box. She pressed her lips together. Was she crying?

No, a giggle escaped. Then Tiffany stifled a laugh. Then Amanda and Max and I let out giggles of relief.

"A pepperoni mountain dog!" exclaimed Shannon.

We all laughed more loudly.

"Why don't you guys come in?" I said.

So the Kilbournes, including Astrid of Grenville, came inside. The five of us sat around the kitchen table and picked at the pizza. Astrid ate all the pieces of pepperoni.

Shannon asked me about the Baby-sitters Club and I told her a little about it. She seemed impressed.

When Max demanded, "Get me a napkin, Shannie," all she had to do was raise an eyebrow at him and he got it himself. Then *I* was impressed. Before the Kilbournes left, I offered to pay for half of the pizza. Shannon grinned. I felt as if, maybe, we were on the way to being friends.

CHAPTER 11

Chicken pocks! The only way your
going to apreciat what I wright here
is if you rember how it felt to have the
chicken packs. I do sort of. I was seven
when I had them and it was not plesent.
I itched and had a feever and my mom
said Don't scratch but it was the only
thing I wanted to do. So keep that in mind.

Ok so malory pike and I sat for her
brothers and sisters. The triplets and
Margoe and claire were all ~~not recov~~
getting over the chicken pax. They were
not felling very good. What a night we
had. Orders, orders, oders. I felt like
there maid. ...

I know this sounds mean, but I'm glad it was Claudia, not I, who had to sit for the Chicken Pox Brigade. There are eight Pike kids, including the triplets, and five of them were sick. I think I'd rather have sat for the Snobs than for kids with chicken pox. (Well, the Snobs don't seem so bad anymore.) Anyway, I did feel sorry for Claudia and Mallory. (Mallory, the oldest Pike, often helps us as a sort of junior baby-sitter when one of us has a job with her family.) They really earned their money that night. They weren't in any danger of catching the chicken pox themselves since they'd both had it, but there were five itchy, unhappy children to take care of, plus Nicky and Vanessa, who seemed unusually cranky.

Mr. and Mrs. Pike had decided to go out to dinner and a movie simply to escape from the chicken pox for awhile. They'd been nursing sick kids all week. Now the five patients were just enough better to be bored. They weren't running fevers, but they were still uncomfortable and had to stay in bed. Mr. and Mrs. Pike needed a break.

"I've set some trays out," Mrs. Pike told Claudia before she and Mr. Pike left. "I'm afraid you'll have to give the triplets, Margo, and

Claire their dinners in bed. Either you or Mallory can eat upstairs with them. The other one can eat downstairs with Nicky and Vanessa."

"Do we have to keep Nicky and Vanessa away from the kids upstairs?" Claudia asked. "I mean, so they don't catch the chicken pox?"

"Oh, no. Don't worry about that," Mrs. Pike replied. "They've been exposed all week. Now, try not to let the sick kids scratch. They're pretty good about it, except for Margo, who scratches every time she thinks we're not looking. Poor thing, she's got a worse case than the others. If any of them complains of a headache, you can give them one children's aspirin. The aspirin is in the medicine cabinet on the very top shelf. Otherwise, just try to keep the kids happy. The portable TV is in the boys' room right now. At seven o'clock, it's the girls' turn to watch it. Mallory can help you with anything else. And the phone numbers are in their usual spot. Okay?"

"Okay," replied Claudia, who was beginning to feel a little apprehensive. Eight Pike kids were one thing; five cases of chicken pox were another.

As soon as Mr. and Mrs. Pike left, Claudia heard a strange little sound, sort of a tinkling noise. "What's that?" she asked Mallory.

She and Mallory were setting up dinner trays for the sick kids.

"What's what?" replied Mallory.

Tinkle-tinkle.

"That," said Claudia.

"Uh-oh! It's the triplets. Mom gave them a bell to ring when they need something. She gave Margo and Claire a triangle."

Ding-ding.

"That wouldn't be the triangle, would it?" asked Claudia.

"Yup," said Mallory, rolling her eyes.

"Well, let's go."

Claudia and Mallory dashed upstairs. Mallory looked in on her brothers while Claudia went to the girls' room. "Hi, you two," she greeted Claire and Margo.

Claire, who is five, put a pitiful expression on her face. "Hi," she said soberly.

"What's the matter?" Claudia asked, concerned.

"We're sick," Claire told her.

"I know. It's too bad."

It really was too bad. Claudia told me that the girls looked pathetic. Their faces and hands — any part of them that wasn't covered by their nightgowns — were a sea of spots. Some of Margo's looked awfully red, and

Claudia suspected that she'd been scratching them.

"We itch," added Margo, who's seven. "Mommy gave us a bath and she put starch in the water to take away the itching, but now it's back again." Her hand drifted toward a spot on her neck, and she touched it so carefully that Claudia couldn't tell whether she was scratching.

"I'm really sorry," said Claudia sympathetically, "but we're going to have fun tonight, and that will take your minds off the itching. In a little while, I'm going to bring your supper upstairs. First I'll eat dinner with you, and then I'll have dessert in the triplets' room — but I'll bring the TV in here. How does that sound?"

"Good," replied Margo and Claire together.

"And now," said Claudia, holding an imaginary microphone to her lips, "for your entertainment pleasure . . . ta-dah! The Kid-Kit!"

Claudia had brought her Kid-Kit to the Pikes' and left it outside the doorway to the girls' room. She carried it in with a flourish and set it on the table between their beds.

"Yea!" cried Claire.

"You guys can play with this stuff until I bring the TV in. Then you can trade, and give the Kid-Kit to the boys, okay?"

"Okay," said Margo, forgetting to scratch as she pawed through the box.

Meanwhile, Mallory had returned to the kitchen and was setting the trays and the table. Further downstairs, in the rec room, eight-year-old Nicky and nine-year-old Vanessa were playing — supposedly. But as Claudia joined Mallory again, she heard Vanessa shriek, "Stop that! You stop that, Nicholas Pike! . . . STOP IT!"

"Whoa," exclaimed Claudia. "I'll go see what that's all about. You finish the trays, okay, Mallory?" She ran downstairs without waiting for a reply. "Hey! What are you two doing?" she cried.

Nicky and Vanessa were sitting on the floor surrounded by Legos. An entire town of Lego buildings had sprung up between them. Claudia couldn't see anything broken or wrong.

"Vanessa?" she asked.

"Nicky gave me the Bizzer Sign!" Vanessa sounded practically hysterical.

"She gave it to me first," grumbled Nicky. "She started it. Honest." He drew a hand wearily across his eyes.

"Did not!" said Vanessa.

"Did, too!"

"Okay, okay," Claudia cut in. Claudia has no patience for the Bizzer sign, which is a hand signal the Pike kids invented purely to annoy each other. "Look, it's almost time for supper. Come on upstairs. You're going to eat in the kitchen with Mallory. A nice, *quiet* meal," she added.

"I'm not hungry," Vanessa whined.

"Me, neither," said Nicky.

"Not even for cream cheese and jelly sandwiches?"

"Well, maybe . . . " Vanessa conceded.

Mallory, Nicky, and Vanessa did eat a quiet, almost somber, meal in the kitchen. Upstairs, Claudia tried to eat with the chicken pox crew, but she hardly had time. No sooner had she settled onto the end of Claire's bed with her tray than she heard *tinkle-tinkle*.

"Coming!" she called, and ran into the triplets' room. "What is it?" she asked the three spotty faces.

"Could we have soda instead of milk?" asked Adam. "Please? It feels so nice and cold."

"Sure," Claudia replied, feeling unduly sorry for them.

She was racing back upstairs with the soda when *ding-ding* sounded from the girls' room. "Coming!" she called. She handed out the sodas rather hastily and dashed back to Claire and Margo.

"Claudia, there's a speck in my cream

cheese," said Margo. "I think it's a bug. If I eat it, I'll throw up."

Claudia examined the speck. "Just a crumb," she pronounced, but to be on the safe side, she picked it out of the cream cheese.

"Could I have some more milk, please?" Claire asked then.

Tinkle-tinkle. The boys were ready for second helpings of fruit salad, and Byron, who loves to eat, wanted dessert, too.

Claudia brought all the food upstairs, then realized it was seven o'clock and time to switch the TV for the Kid-Kit. She did so, wolfed down part of her sandwich, then began carrying the trays to the kitchen so she could help Mallory clean up.

The bell and the triangle were quiet for a full five minutes before Jordan asked for an aspirin for his headache. It was during the next lull that Claudia peered down into the rec room to see what Vanessa and Nicky were up to. She saw them both sitting in front of the TV, their shirts pulled up, examining their tummies and chests. "What are you doing?" she called.

"Counting," Nicky called back.

"Counting what?"

"Our spots."

"Uh-oh," said Claudia, and she dashed

downstairs to find that, just as she'd feared, poor Mr. and Mrs. Pike had two new chicken pox patients.

"Bedtime, you guys," she announced, and neither one objected.

CHAPTER 12

Louie was in bad shape. Everyone could see it. Even David Michael. He didn't understand it, but he could see it.

"He's falling apart," Mom said one Saturday as she and Louie returned home from a trip to the vet. "He's simply old. Nothing is working very well anymore."

It was true. Louie had lots of accidents now, so we had to keep him in the kitchen and the family room, where there were no Oriental rugs. His arthritis was worse, and we could tell he was in a lot of pain. He didn't move unless he had to, and when he did, it was a big effort. Now, instead of calling Louie for dinner, David Michael brought dinner to him.

"After all," said my brother, "when I'm sick, Mom brings me my meals on a tray, so I'm kind of doing the same thing for Louie."

Even though he didn't feel well, Louie tried to be the same good old collie as always. For instance, he usually tried to get to his feet and over to the back door so somebody could let him out before he had an accident. It's just that often he didn't make it. He was too slow. One day, the day before Mom took him back to Dr. Smith, he staggered to his feet as David Michael was approaching him with his dinner.

"You need to go out, Louie?" my brother asked. "Okay, hold on a sec." David Michael set the bowl down. He went off in search of his slicker since it had begun to rain, and returned to the kitchen in time to see Louie's hindquarters disappear through the open basement doorway.

"Louie!" David Michael cried. "No! Wait!"

Ever since Dr. Smith had told us about Louie's eyesight, we'd tried to keep the door to the basement closed, but now and then one of us would forget. It just hadn't become a habit yet. Which was too bad, because a steep flight of fourteen stone steps led from that doorway into the dark cellar below.

David Michael grabbed for the banister with one hand and Louie's collar with the other, even though Louie had already stumbled down the first couple of steps. Thank goodness Louie moves slowly, otherwise he probably would have fallen headlong to the bottom of the stairs. As it was, he and David Michael fell several more steps together and David Michael banged his face on the banister and wound up with a black eye.

It was that accident that prompted Mom to take Louie to Dr. Smith the next day. And it was at that visit that Dr. Smith said Louie was deteriorating rapidly (translated into regular speech, that meant "getting worse fast"), and suggested injections. I hadn't gone with Mom to the vet and didn't ask what the injections were for. I didn't really want to understand. All I did know was that Dr. Smith said she could try a last resort with Louie — she would give him special injections two times *every day*.

Needless to say, this was not easy to fit into our schedule, although of course we agreed that it must be done, since no schedule was more important than Louie. We finally worked out a plan where Mom left the house early and drove Louie to Dr. Smith's for his first injection of the day, while Watson took care of breakfast and seeing us Thomas kids off to school. Then Mom dropped Louie back at the house and arrived at her office fifteen minutes later than usual. On Monday and Wednesday afternoons, Charlie sped home from school, picked Louie up, drove him to Dr. Smith's for his *second* injection, sped home, dropped Louie off, picked me up, and drove me to my Baby-sitters Club meeting. On Tuesday and Thursday, when Charlie was busy, Watson skipped lunch, and used his "lunch hour" in the middle of the afternoon to take Louie to Dr. Smith. The new schedule was hectic, Mom and Watson and Charlie were harried by it, and worst of all, by Friday, after almost a week of injections, Dr. Smith admitted to Charlie that they weren't helping Louie much — and that the two car trips every day were too much for him.

Charlie was upset by the news, and so was I, when he told me about it as we settled Louie into the kitchen. In fact, I was so worried that I actually called Claudia to tell her I wouldn't be able to make our Friday club meeting. Dawn, as our alternate officer, would have to take over my duties as president.

It was a good thing I didn't go. If I had, I wouldn't have been around for all the commotion that was about to happen. Even though in a big family, especially a stepfamily, you learn to expect commotion, I wasn't prepared for what was to follow. Things started when Watson and his ex-wife somehow got their signals crossed and the first Mrs. Brewer dropped Karen and Andrew off earlier than usual for their weekend with us, thinking that Watson was home. He wasn't, but it was okay since Charlie and David Michael and I were.

Karen ran inside, full of energy, with Andrew at her heels. "Hi, everybody!" she called. "Here we are!" She dropped her knapsack and a tote bag in the front hall by the staircase. Andrew dropped his things on Karen's.

"What's for dinner?" asked Karen. "Where's Boo-Boo? Have you seen Morbidda Destiny? How's Louie?"

Karen usually leaves the rest of us in shock with her talk and excitement and enthusiasm. For the next half hour we were one step behind her as she and Andrew settled into the routine at their dad's house. First Karen ran to one of the windows that faces Mrs. Porter's house next door.

"Eeee!" she screeched. "I can see her! I can see her in her kitchen. She's mixing something in a pot. You know what I think?"

(By this time the rest of us, including quiet Andrew, had gathered behind Karen and were peering at Mrs. Porter.)

"I think she's mixing a wicked witch's brew! She's stirring up a brew that's going to grow fur all over Andrew or — "

"Dope," said Charlie fondly, clapping a hand over Karen's mouth. He smiled at her and shook his head. "You know she can't do stuff like that. She's probably making soup."

"Kristy?" asked Andrew, turning a worried face to me.

"Oh, Andrew," I said, kneeling down, "you're not going to grow fur. Don't give it a second thought."

By this time, Karen was already gone. She'd run into Watson's den and found Boo-Boo asleep in a leather armchair. (I swear, that cat always picks the most uncomfortable spots for his naps.) And she summoned us from the window with another shriek.

"He's growing fangs! Boo-Boo is growing fangs!" Karen was crying as we caught up with her. "It's Morbidda Destiny again."

I was positive, no matter what Karen said, and no matter what doubts I have about our next-door neighbor, that Boo-Boo was not growing fangs. I tiptoed to the leather chair while everyone else looked on in silence. Despite Karen's shrieking a moment earlier, Boo-Boo was still sound asleep. He was sprawled on his back, and was, in fact, *so* sound asleep, that his mouth was slightly open. I saw why Karen thought he had fangs.

Smiling, I tiptoed back to her. "Those aren't fangs," I said, with a laugh. "They're just his regular old teeth. They're called incisors or something. I guess you never noticed them before. Look, even humans have them." I opened my mouth and showed her my four pointy teeth.

"Whew," breathed Karen. "I was worried . . . I wonder if Louie has those teeth, too." And she was off again.

Her third screech came from the kitchen.

"What now?" asked Charlie wearily. We were getting tired of Karen's games. But her third screech was followed by a fourth, and both sounded truly terrified.

"Oh, boy," I said under my breath.

Charlie, David Michael, Andrew, and I ran to the kitchen. The four of us skidded to a halt behind Karen. For a moment, no one spoke. We just stared at Louie. I couldn't believe what he was doing.

David Michael began to cry. I turned him away from Louie and hugged him to me.

Charlie drew in his breath and approached Louie, while I tried to turn Karen and Andrew around and hug my brother at the same time.

Luckily, Mom and Watson both arrived home just then. I hoped one of them would know what to do.

Louie seemed to have lost complete control of his hind legs. He was pulling himself around the kitchen with his front legs, dragging the back ones as if they were paralyzed. And he was, as you might imagine, in a panic. He crawled into a leg of the kitchen table, and then into the stove.

"Lou-ie!" David Michael howled.

"Charlie, take David Michael out of the kitchen," my mother ordered.

"Please take Karen and Andrew, too," added Watson.

Charlie did as he was told, but nobody had asked me to do anything, so I just stood by the doorway and watched.

Mom ran for the phone and dialed Dr. Smith while Watson tried to calm Louie down. He succeeded somewhat, and I relaxed a little and tried to figure out what the phone conversation was about, but all Mom would say was "Mm-hmm," and, "Yes, that's right," and, "I see," and finally, "Okay, thank you." When she got off the phone, she turned to me. "Kristy, tell the others we'll have a family meeting as soon as Sam comes home."

That family meeting is something I wish I could forget, but know I'll never be able to. The eight of us — Mom, Watson, Charlie, Sam, David Michael, Andrew, Karen, and I — gathered in the living room.

Mom said bluntly, "Kids, I'm sorry to have to tell you this, but Louie is very, very sick now. And he's not going to get better."

Charlie and Sam and I lowered our heads. But David Michael, Andrew, and Karen looked at Mom with wide, surprised eyes.

"What about the shots? And the pills?" asked my little brother.

"They're not working," Mom told him. "You can see that, can't you, honey?"

David Michael nodded, his eyes filling with tears.

"So what do we do now?" asked Sam.

Mom glanced at Watson and I could see that *her* eyes were teary, too. Watson took her hand reassuringly. "Dr. Smith suggested that we have Louie put down tomorrow," he said gently.

I expected my brothers to get angry, to yell that *nobody* would *ever* do that to Louie. But they all began to cry instead. David Michael cried noisily. Sam and Charlie tried to hide the fact that they were crying, but I know they were. Then a lump that had been filling up my throat all afternoon, dissolved, and I began to cry, too, which made Andrew and Karen burst into tears. It didn't matter. Even Watson was crying.

After a few moments, David Michael announced, "I'm going to sleep with Louie tonight." We knew he meant sleep in the family room with him, and I'm sure he thought some-

116

one was going to try to stop him, but no one said a word.

So Louie and David Michael spent the night together. Just as Louie had often joined one of us in bed, to keep us company, David Michael kept Louie company during his last night with us.

CHAPTER 13

Mom said it wasn't necessary for all of us to go to Dr. Smith's the next day, and I worried that we would argue about who stayed and who went. Sam and Charlie looked relieved, though, and said they wouldn't mind staying home. (I think they were afraid they'd cry at the vet's, and that people would see them.) Watson then asked if my brothers would watch Karen and Andrew. He'd decided they were too young to go. Sam and Charlie agreed right away. And that's how Mom and Watson, David Michael, and I became the four who accompanied Louie to the vet.

David Michael had spent an uncomfortable night with Louie. He'd insisted on sleeping next to him, on the floor. He wouldn't even consider the couch. Louie whined a lot that night, according to Mom, who (although David Michael didn't know it) spent most of the night reading in the kitchen, keeping her ears open for problems in the family room. But toward dawn, both Louie and my brother fell asleep. They stayed asleep until nine o'clock when Mom reluctantly woke David Michael. She wanted to get the trip to Dr. Smith's over with as soon as possible.

At breakfast that morning nobody ate much. And we were silent. Nobody even asked for a reprieve for Louie. He was just in too much pain. We knew that giving Louie an extra day or two would be one of the cruelest things we could do to him.

At ten-thirty, David Michael and I wrapped Louie in his blanket and Watson placed him on the backseat of our station wagon. Karen and Andrew looked on in awe.

"Do you want to say good-bye?" Watson asked them.

Karen stepped forward solemnly, ducked into the car, lifted Louie's ear, and whispered into it, "Good-bye, Louie." Then she fled to the house in tears.

But Andrew called gaily, " 'Bye, Louie!" and I realized that he was too little to understand what was happening. Or maybe he was able to see the good that we were doing Louie easier than the rest of us were.

Charlie and Sam asked to say good-bye in private. When they returned to the house to watch Andrew and Karen, the rest of us reluctantly climbed into the car. I squinched up in the very back part of the station wagon so that David Michael could sit next to Louie.

Nobody spoke during the drive to the vet's, but David Michael held one of Louie's paws the whole way. And Louie, our noisy vet-hater, didn't so much as whimper, even though he must have known he was going to Dr. Smith's. After all, he'd been there ten times in the past five days.

When we reached the vet's, Watson parked the car. Then he lifted Louie out and handed him to Mom. Watson had decided to let us Thomases take Louie inside by ourselves. He hadn't known Louie the way we had.

We walked slowly to the door to the veterinary offices, and David Michael held it open for Mom, while I reached into my pocket, pulled out a pair of sunglasses, and put them on so nobody would see my red eyes.

Five other people were in the waiting room, but the receptionist called to us right away. "Dr. Smith is seeing a patient now," she said, "but as soon as she's done, you can go in."

My mother nodded. Then she turned to me. "Kristy, I want you and David Michael to say good-bye out here. I'm the only one who needs to go inside. Do you understand?"

120

"Yes," I whispered. I began stroking Louie's muzzle.

"How do they put him to sleep?" asked David Michael tearfully.

"They just give him a shot," replied my mother. "That's all. It'll make him go to sleep and he won't wake up."

Mom had sat down on a couch in the waiting room with Louie stretched across her lap. Several people looked at us sympathetically. One elderly woman began to sniffle and dab at her eyes with a tissue.

"Will you hold him while he gets the shot?" asked David Michael. "I want you to hold him."

"Yes, I promise," said Mom. "That's why I'm going in. To be with him."

I looked down at Louie's liquid brown eyes. When he moved them, his "eyebrows" moved, too. He was paying attention to everything in the waiting room.

"Do you think he knows what's going to happen?" I asked softly.

"No," said Mom. "I'm sure he doesn't."

How can we do this to him? I asked myself. We are going to kill him. We were saying, "Okay, Louie, you must die now," and not giving him any choice about it. We were going to send him into a room and let someone give him a shot so that he would never wake up.

But then I remembered what he had looked like the night before, and how much he was hurting, and knew we were doing the right thing.

The receptionist called Mom's name then, and she stood up. David Michael and I gave Louie last pats and kisses, and then Mom disappeared down the little hallway. When she came back a few minutes later, her arms were empty.

Karen said the funeral was her idea, but I think it was Watson's. At any rate, later that day, right after lunch, Karen found David Michael and me sitting glumly in front of the TV set. We didn't even know what we were watching.

"I think we should have a funeral for Louie," Karen announced.

"A funeral?" I repeated.

"Yes. To remember him by."

I glanced at David Michael, who seemed to have perked up.

"We could make a gravestone," he said. "Even though we can't really bury him."

"And we can sing a song and say some nice things about him," added Karen. "We'll hold it at three o'clock. I'll go tell everyone."

Right away, we began making plans. All six

of us kids gathered on the back porch.

"What kind of marker should we make for his grave?" I asked. "I don't think we have any stone."

"A wooden cross," said Karen decisively. "There are some scraps of wood in the shed."

"We can take care of that," said Sam, speaking for himself and Charlie. I could tell they were just humoring us. They felt bad about Louie, but they felt too old to be planning pet funerals, and wanted to go off on their own.

"Put 'Louie Thomas, R.I.P.' on the cross," instructed Karen.

"What's 'R.I.P.'?" asked David Michael.

"It means 'rest in peace.' "

"Shouldn't we write that out?" I asked. "Initials are tacky. It's like writing 'Xmas' instead of 'Christmas.' "

"No!" cried Karen, who's been wanting to have her own way a lot lately. "Put 'R.I.P.' That's how it always is in books and on TV."

Karen and I had a big discussion about the matter. Sam finally came to the rescue by suggesting that he and Charlie write 'Rest In Peace' with huge initial letters so the R, the I, and the P would really show up. Then they left David Michael, Karen, Andrew, and me to plan the rest of the service.

"We should sing a hymn," said David Michael.

But none of us knew any hymns by heart, except for Christmas carols.

"How about singing a song about a dog?" I suggested.

"I know one," said Andrew, and he began to sing, "There was a farmer, had a dog, and Bingo was his name-o. B-I-N-G-O — "

"We can't sing that at a funeral!" David Michael exclaimed.

"Old MacDonald?" said Andrew. "On his farm he could have a dog."

"*No.*"

"Let's just sing a sad song," said Karen.

"No, a happy one," I said. "Louie wouldn't want us all to be sad."

"But funerals are *supposed* to be sad," she insisted.

We talked and talked. Finally we reached a few decisions. Instead of singing a song, we voted to play "Brother Louie" on the tape deck. Then we decided that we would each say one nice thing about Louie, instead of having someone give a boring eulogy. Saying nice things was Andrew's idea. His nursery-school teacher had just read his class a book called *The Tenth Good Thing About Barney*, in which a family remembers their pet, Barney, after he dies. (I thought it was very lucky that Andrew had heard that story just before Louie died.)

At ten minutes to three, us six Thomas/Brewer kids called Mom and Watson, and our family walked out to the backyard and stood by a forsythia bush Louie had liked to sleep near. Sam was holding the cross he and Charlie had made, Charlie was holding a shovel, and David Michael was holding Louie's leash and food dishes. We were going to bury them under the cross. That was, we'd decided, almost like burying Louie himself.

"Okay," I said. "Charlie, why don't you dig the grave? Then we can say the nice things about Louie."

"No!" cried Karen. "Not everyone's here."

"Yes, we are," I told her. "Eight people. We're all here."

Just then I heard someone say, "Are we late?"

I turned around. Filing into our yard were Shannon and Tiffany, Hannie and Linny, and Amanda and Max. They were followed by two of Shannon's snobby friends. They gathered behind our family.

I looked at Karen in horror.

"I invited them," she said simply.

I shook my head. I didn't want Shannon at Louie's funeral. She'd made fun of him. Besides, what would she think about a dog funeral? But there was nothing to do except go ahead with it.

Charlie, red with embarrassment at the sight of our guests, finished digging the grave. David Michael stepped forward and placed the leash and the dishes in it. Then Sam covered them up and pushed the cross into the earth.

"Now," said David Michael, "we each say one nice thing. I'll go last."

Karen, of course, volunteered to go first, and said, "Louie had good manners."

"He slept on my feet to keep them warm," said Andrew.

I dared to turn around and peek at the rest of the audience. To my surprise, not a single person was laughing. And Shannon was wiping tears away.

"Louie was a good football player," said Charlie.

"He had a sense of humor," I said.

"He was good company," said Sam.

"He was an adorable puppy," said Mom.

"He was nice to Boo-Boo," said Watson.

David Michael let out a sigh. "He was my best friend," he said.

After a moment of silence, David Michael pushed a button on the tape deck, and "Brother Louie" came on. We all thought of our good old collie while "Louie, Louie, Louie" was sung.

When the song was over, I felt both happy and sad. A hand touched my arm. It was Shannon. "I'm really sorry about Louie," she said seriously. "If anything happened to Astrid, I don't know what I'd do." Then she turned away, and Louie's mourners began to leave.

CHAPTER 14

It was on Monday, two days after Louie's funeral, that I sat for the Snobs again. I didn't really think the Delaneys were so bad anymore, but the name had stuck.

"Tell us again what happened to Louie," said Max.

He and Amanda and I were playing Snail in the driveway, but the Snobs kept stopping to ask questions about Louie. They weren't being rude; they were just curious. They'd probably never known anyone or anything that had died.

"Louie was sick," I said for the fourth or fifth time. "He was really old and he didn't feel well anymore. He hurt a lot. . . . Your turn, Amanda."

Amanda hopped to the center of the snail shell, expertly avoiding Max's and my squares. She selected a square for herself and drew an

"A" in it. "How did Louie fall down the stairs?" she wanted to know.

"He couldn't see them. He just walked right down."

I stood at the edge of the shell and hopped around and around to the center. Amanda handed me the chalk.

"And David Michael banged his eye?" said Max.

"Yup," I replied, choosing another square.

"Did he cry?"

"A little. His eye turned black and blue."

"Priscilla has never been sick," said Amanda. "I think it's because she cost four hundred dollars."

"Well, I doubt that," I told her, "but I'm glad she's so healthy."

"If Priscilla dies," said Max, "let's give her a funeral."

Amanda scrunched up her face in thought. "Okay," she replied. "We could make a cross for her. And we could play music from *The Aristocats*."

"And I," said Max, "would say, 'Priscilla had a beautiful tail.' "

"And I'd say, 'Priscilla cost four hundred dollars,' " added Amanda.

I rolled my eyes.

Amanda was taking her turn again, when

Shannon Kilbourne rounded a corner of the Delaneys' house and walked over to us. She was cradling something in her arms.

"Hi," I said uncertainly. I didn't dislike Shannon anymore, I just never knew what to expect from her.

"Hi," she replied cheerfully. "This is for you." She held out the thing she'd brought over.

"Oh!" I squealed. I couldn't believe it. The "thing" was a puppy! A very tiny puppy, probably only a few weeks old.

"What do you mean he's for me?" I exclaimed. "Where'd you get him? Where'd he come from?"

"*He's* a *she*," replied Shannon, "and she's one of Astrid's."

"One of Astrid's? You mean one of Astrid of Grenville's *puppies?* But I thought Astrid was a boy."

Shannon grinned. "No!" she cried. "Astrid is a girl's name. It's Scandinavian or something. It means divine strength."

I just couldn't believe it. Why was Shannon giving me a puppy? None of this made sense.

"I don't know why I assumed Astrid was a boy, but I did. How come you never told me she has puppies?" I asked.

"I don't know. You never asked. The subject never came up. Anyway, we — I mean, Tiffany and Maria and my parents and I — want you to have this puppy. It's purebred. We're selling the others. But we really want your family to have this one. You know . . . because of Louie . . ." Shannon's voice trailed off.

"Thank you," I said softly. I looked down at the fat little puppy that was nestled in my arms. She was a ball of brown and white fluff. When I leaned over to nuzzle her, she licked my nose.

"I'm afraid you can't have her yet," said Shannon. "She's only six weeks old. We want the puppies to stay with Astrid until they're eight weeks. But then she's all yours. If it's okay with Mr. Br — with your parents."

"Well, I'll have to check with them, but I'm sure it'll be all right. They loved having Louie around. The one I'm worried about is David Michael. I don't know what he'll think about getting a 'replacement' for Louie. Or at least, getting a replacement so soon."

"Well, why don't you find out?" asked Shannon. "Is he home? Tell him to come over here and meet the puppy."

"I better phone my mom first," I said.

"Shannie, Shannie!" cried Amanda, jumping up and down. "Can we please play with the puppy?"

"Please, please, puh-*lease*?" added Max.

It was the first time I'd heard the Snobs say please on their own. I wasn't sure whether they were really being polite, or whether they just wanted to ensure that they'd be allowed to play with the puppy. Either way, it sounded nice.

"You can play with the puppy," Shannon replied, "but we have to take her inside. There are lots of germs outside, and she hasn't had her shots yet."

"Oh," said Amanda. "Well, is she going to wet or anything? We have to be careful. The fountain in the hallway cost two thousand dollars. And the rugs in the living room are genuine Oriental, and *they* cost —"

"Amanda," I interrupted her, "don't worry about it. We'll keep the puppy in the kitchen, and we'll put newspapers on the floor first.

Shannon, the Snobs, the puppy, and I went into the Delaneys' house through the back door (to avoid the two thousand-dollar fountain). While I sat in a kitchen chair with the puppy in my lap, Shannon and the Snobs covered the floor with newspapers. Then I put the puppy down and let her frisk around. She pretended to act fearless and would stalk enemy chair legs and cupboard doors, but when Priscilla appeared, the puppy jumped a mile. Priscilla, startled, jumped a mile, too. She fled to the top of the refrigerator while the puppy fled to a corner.

Amanda and Max giggled hysterically.

"Here," said Shannon. "Throw the rubber steak to her, Max."

Shannon had produced a chewed-up rubber toy, and Max tossed it across the room. The puppy ran after it on fat legs, skidding on the paper.

"Well, what do you think of her?" Shannon asked me.

"I think she's adorable," I replied, "but I better get on the phone."

I dialed my mother at her office. "Mom!" I exclaimed. "You'll never guess what! Shannon Kilbourne — you know, from across the street? Well, her dog had puppies, little baby Bernese mountain dogs, and she brought one over to the Delaneys', that's where I'm baby-sitting, and said we can have her — it's a she — because of Louie. But we can't have her for two weeks." I hadn't given my mom a chance to say a word, because I'd suddenly realized how much I didn't want her to say "no." I'd realized what a thoroughly nice thing Shannon was doing, and that it could only mean she wanted to be friends. "Could we please have the puppy, Mom?" I asked, slowing down and trying to sound more grown up. "I think it would be good for David Michael. And if he doesn't like the idea, we'll still have two weeks to convince him. In two —"

"Kristy," my mother finally interrupted me, "we can have the dog."

"We *can?*" I squeaked.

"Yes. Watson and I had already decided to get another dog as soon as we thought David Michael was ready. We were even thinking about buying one of the Kilbournes' puppies, so I know this will be okay with Watson. I'll call the Kilbournes tonight to thank them."

"*You* knew Astrid was a girl, too?" was all I could exclaim. "You knew about the puppies?"

Of course, Mom had no idea why I said that, and she was in a rush to get back to work, so we ended the conversation. Boy, I thought when I'd hung up the phone, I must really be out of it. I decided this was my punishment for thinking that all my neighbors were snobs, and not bothering to get to know them.

"Mom said yes!" I announced to Shannon.

"Great," she replied. "Now call your brother."

I did, but I didn't tell him why I was calling. I just asked him to come over to the Delaneys'.

While we waited for David Michael, Amanda and Max played with the puppy. "You know,"

I said to Shannon as we watched the kids, "I'm really sorry about taking your baby-sitting jobs away from you. I baby-sat so much in my old neighborhood that it didn't occur to me *not* to sit when I moved here. It's just part of my life. I didn't think about the people here who might already be sitters."

"Oh, that's okay," replied Shannon. "There are more than enough jobs to go around. Tiffany and I are the only ones of our friends who really like to baby-sit, and we can't possibly do it all ourselves. I don't think I was mad at you as much as I was . . ." (Shannon blushed) ". . . jealous."

"Jealous of *me?*"

"Yeah. Because your club is such a good idea."

"But you and Tiffany kind of implied that our club is babyish."

"Yeah, we did. But we didn't mean it."

The doorbell rang then and I let David Michael in. When he saw the puppy on the kitchen floor a whole range of expressions crossed his face. First he looked surprised, then pleased, then sad (thinking of Louie, I guess), and then wary.

"Whose is that?" he asked. He looked from Shannon to the Snobs.

"Actually, she's ours," I answered. "If you

want her." I told him about the Kilbournes' offer.

"I don't want her," David Michael said rudely, and I felt like shaking him. "She isn't Louie." But before I could do anything, David Michael knelt down on the floor, in spite of himself.

The puppy pranced over to him and stood with her front feet on my brother's knees. David Michael smiled.

Shannon and I looked at each other and smiled, too.

The puppy stretched up, David Michael leaned over, and they touched noses.

"Ooh," said David Michael, "she has a soft nozzle."

"Muzzle," I corrected him.

"If we keep her," said my brother, "she won't be Louie. Louie was special."

"No," I agreed. "Louie was one-of-a-kind. This puppy is a girl, and she'll look different and act different. She's not a new Louie."

"Good," said David Michael.

"So do you want her?" asked Shannon.

"Yes," replied my brother.

"And what do you say?" I prompted him.

"I say, 'Let's name her Shannon.' "

So we did.

CHAPTER 15

"Help! Kristy! Save me! The ghost of Ben Brewer is after me!"

Karen ran shrieking through the second-floor hallway and burst into my room in a panic. "Kristy! Kristy!"

"Ahem, Karen," I replied.

Karen was only fooling around. She knew as well as I did that there probably wasn't any ghost in our attic. And if there was (because we just weren't *sure*) he certainly wasn't going to chase little girls around in broad daylight.

It was a Saturday afternoon, two weeks to the day since Louie's funeral. Karen and Andrew were spending another weekend with us, and Shannon the puppy was almost ours. The members of the Baby-sitters Club were gathered in my room. We'd just had a meeting the day before, of course, but every now and then we like to get together and *not* conduct business. Besides, my friends enjoy visiting the mansion.

Karen plopped down on the floor between Mary Anne and Dawn. "You know who old Ben Brewer is, don't you?" she asked them.

"Your great-grandfather?" Mary Anne ventured. (Ghost stories make her nervous.)

"Right. Before he became a ghost, anyway. He was a — what's the word, Kristy?"

"Herpitologist?" I suggested.

"*No!*" cried Karen, laughing. "The word that means he stayed in the house all alone for years. He never went out and no one ever went in."

"He was a recluse," I said, "according to Brewer family history."

"And he ate fried dandelions," Karen added. Stacey snorted.

"Well, he *did*," Karen insisted, turning to Stacey indignantly. "Anyway, he's a ghost now and he haunts our attic."

"Only the attic?" asked Claudia.

"Yes, thank goodness," I replied.

"But every now and then he leaves it," said Karen. "Just for a few minutes. He likes to chase me through the halls. He says otherwise he never gets any exercise."

"You mean any e-x-o-r-c-i-s-e?" spelled Mary Anne, but Karen wasn't old enough to get the joke. The rest of us laughed, though.

"You do know that's not true, don't you, Karen?" I asked.

"Yes," she admitted. "But it's fun to pretend. Sometimes I'm *sure* he's behind me." (I shivered.) "But it's not pretend about the attic. He really haunts it."

"We have an honest-to-goodness secret passage in our house," spoke up Dawn.

"You do?" Karen's eyes widened.

"I've been in it," I announced.

"You *have?*" Karen's eyes became the size of soup tureens.

Crash, bang, THUMP.

"What was that?" exclaimed Stacey.

"My brothers," I replied. "I think."

"Yup, that's right," said Karen. "They're playing football."

"In the house?" I asked.

"Yes. Andrew is the football."

I rolled my eyes. Mom and Watson were out for the afternoon. I wasn't baby-sitting, since Sam and Charlie were home, but I felt I should be on top of things. There were ten kids in the house, plus Boo-Boo.

"This house," I informed my friends, "is actually a *mad*house. Can you imagine what it'll be like when Shannon arrives?"

At that moment, Charlie charged into my

room with Andrew in his arms and threw him on the bed. "Touchdown!" he shouted.

Andrew squealed and giggled. He sounded a little *too* wild, which was unlike him. "Do a cannonball!" he shrieked. He tucked himself into a ball and Charlie picked him up again and ran him down the hall chanting, "Ba-boom-ba-boom-ba-boom-ba-boom." We heard a soft thud as my brother tossed him onto another bed.

"Hey, you guys! Perk up!" I shouted to them. My friends laughed.

Karen ran after Charlie shouting, "My turn! My turn!"

"When do you get Shannon?" Mary Anne wanted to know.

"In two or three days," I replied.

"You know, Kristy," Claudia began, "I hate to say this, but — "

"Then don't," I interrupted.

"Don't what?"

"Say it."

Claudia made a face at me. *"But,"* she continued, "you complained an awful lot about Shannon Kilbourne and the other snobby girls around here, and now Shannon's giving you a puppy. That's a pretty nice thing to do."

"I know," I said in a small voice as I traced the pattern of the bedspread with my finger.

"She's not as bad as I thought she was. In fact, she's sort of all right."

"Well, what happened?" asked Dawn.

I shook my head. "I'm not sure. But we did have a talk the day Shannon brought Shannon to meet me."

"What kind of talk?" asked Claudia. She was lying on her back on the floor and began blowing a gigantic pink bubble with a wad of Bazooka.

"You know, if that pops, it's going to cover your face and goo up your hair," Stacey pointed out after a few seconds.

Claudia ignored her and kept on blowing.

"We had a very pleasant talk," I replied. "We talked about baby-sitting. I said I hadn't realized that I might be stepping on someone else's territory when I started sitting around here. It was just *natural* for me to sit."

"What did Shannon say?" asked Mary Anne. "Did she understand?"

"Oh, yes. Believe it or not, she said she was *jealous*."

"You're kidding," said Dawn and Stacey at the same time.

"Nope. She said she wasn't really mad, because she and Tiffany — that's her sister — are the only ones who are interested in sitting, and there are more than enough jobs for them in this neighborhood. But she's jealous of our club."

"I wonder," said Mary Anne slowly, "if she'd want to be another associate member of the club. Like Logan is. We can always use extra people to call on when we're too busy."

"Yeah," I agreed. "And that way she could be part of the club without actually joining it."

"Why shouldn't we ask her to *join?*" wondered Stacey. "It wasn't too long ago that we were so busy we wanted new members. Of course, we'd have to meet her first."

I looked at the rest of my friends. Except for Claudia, they were shrugging and nodding, as if to say, "Why not?" Claudia was still blowing her bubble. Very, very slowly, it was becoming an award-winning size.

"I'll call Shannon," I said. And did. Shannon's mother informed me that Shannon just happened to be on her way over, bringing Shannon to visit with David Michael.

"That's perfect," I told the club members, after I'd hung up. "Shannon the puppy can play with David Michael. Shannon the baby-sitter can meet you guys."

This seemed like an ideal plan — except that Shannon the baby-sitter entered my room just as three things happened: Claudia's bubble popped (and, as predicted, covered her face and gooed up her hair), Stacey spilled a soda, and Charlie cannonballed Andrew onto my bed.

Shannon looked around as if she'd just entered the loony bin.

"Hi!" I called nervously. I passed tissues to Stacey while Charlie and Andrew crashed out of the room. I closed the door after them.

Claudia sat up, picking pink shreds out of her eyelashes.

"Um, meet the Baby-sitters Club," I said. "The normal ones are Dawn and Mary Anne. The sticky ones are Claudia and Stacey. This is Shannon Kilbourne, everyone."

There was nothing to do but laugh. So we did.

"Are you having a club meeting?" asked Shannon when we'd calmed down.

"Not really," I said. "We hold our meetings during the week. On Mondays, Wednesdays, and Fridays from five-thirty until six," I added. (I might as well fill her in on the workings of the club.)

"You meet that often?" she replied, sounding impressed. "Gosh. I could never do that."

I exchanged a look with Stacey. "How come?" I asked.

"Oh, tons of reasons. Homework. After-school stuff. I'm usually pretty busy. I could never be so, you know, committed to something. This club must mean a lot to you."

"Oh, it does," I assured her.

"You're sure you couldn't commit to the club?" Stacey asked.

"Yeah," answered Shannon, puzzled. "How come?"

"Well," I said, "we'd been wondering if you'd like to join. Lots of times we get more jobs than we can handle. And clients like to get baby-sitters who live in their own neighborhood so they don't have to pick them up and take them home. I'm the only club member who lives around here. We thought you'd be a good addition to the Baby-sitters Club."

Shannon looked both pained and thoughtful. "I'd really *like* to join," she said, "but I just don't see how."

"Well," Mary Anne jumped in, wanting to make her feel better, "listen, don't worry. You could be an associate member of the club. We already have one and we could use another. That would be perfect for you because associate members don't have to attend meetings. We just call them and offer them any jobs we can't take. You earn some extra money, maybe find some new kids to sit for, and we keep our clients satisfied by always being able to provide them with sitters."

We looked expectantly at Shannon. "What do you think?" I asked her.

"I think it sounds fabulous," she replied. "I accept."

"Yea!" I cried. "Shannon is our new associate member of the Baby-sitters Club."

"You asked a *dog* to join your club?" spoke up an amazed voice.

My friends and I turned to see David Michael standing in the doorway, holding Shannon the puppy awkwardly, her hind legs dangling.

"No, silly!" I exclaimed. "The other Shannon. Shannon the human."

"Oh," he replied, and set Shannon on the floor. The puppy frisked into my room and David Michael followed her, smiling happily.

I knew David Michael would never forget our Louie. None of us would, because Louie had left a sort of legacy. He'd brought Shannon and me together so we could be friends instead of enemies, and that in turn had brought a new puppy for our family, but especially for David Michael. So, I thought. Endings could sometimes be beginnings. They were sad, but sometimes they brought happiness.

That's what Louie had shown us, and that's just one of the things we would remember about him.

About the Author

ANN M. MARTIN did *a lot* of baby-sitting when she was growing up in Princeton, New Jersey. Now her favorite baby-sitting charge is her cat, Mouse, who lives with her in her Manhattan apartment.

Ann Martin's Apple Paperbacks are *Bummer Summer, Inside Out, Stage Fright, Me and Katie (the Pest),* and all the other books in the Baby-sitters Club series.

She is a former editor of books for children, and was graduated from Smith College. She likes ice cream, the beach, and *I Love Lucy;* and she hates to cook.

Look for #12

CLAUDIA AND THE NEW GIRL

"Mm-hmm." Mrs. Hall looked slightly disappointed. "And have you read *The Yearling*? Or *A Tree Grows in Brooklyn*?" I could tell she was thinking of transferring Ashley to one of the other English classes.

Ashley nodded. "I read them over the summer. But I don't mind doing the Newbery books again. I mean, we didn't read *all* of them. There are too many. Maybe I could do a special project on some of the older ones. The ones from the nineteen-thirties, if that's okay."

Mrs. Hall looked impressed. I was pretty impressed myself. What kind of kid got away with suggesting work to a teacher?

When class was over, Ashley and I looked at each other again. Then Ashley said quietly, "Um, hi. Do you know where room two-six-teen is?" It sounded as if it were killing her to have to talk to me. She certainly wasn't the friendliest person I'd ever met.

"Sure," I answered. "It's on the way to my math class. I'll take you."

"Oh, okay. . . . Thanks."

Ashley and I edged into the crowded hallway and headed for a staircase.

"My name's Claudia," I told her. "Claudia Kishi. Um, I was wondering. I know this sounds funny, but are you related to Andrew Wyeth?"

"No," replied Ashley. She paused, as if deciding whether to say anything else. Then she added, "I wish I were, though."

So she knew who I meant!

"Boy, so do I," I told her.

"Do you like his work?" asked Ashley. She glanced at me, then quickly looked away.

"*Like* it? I love it! I take all kinds of art classes. I want to be a painter some day. Or a sculptress. Or maybe a potter."

"You do?" said Ashley. "So do I. I mean, I want to be a sculptress."

She was going to say something more then, but the warning bell rang and we had to duck into our classrooms. Before I did, though, I glanced once more at Ashley's retreating figure. I knew that somebody very . . . different had walked into my life.

Here's some news about other books in The Baby-sitters Club series by Ann M. Martin

#1 *Kristy's Great Idea*

Kristy thinks the Baby-sitters Club is a great idea. She and her friends Claudia, Stacey, and Mary Anne all love taking care of kids. But nobody counted on crank calls, wild pets, and uncontrollable two-year-olds! Having a Baby-sitters Club isn't easy, but Kristy and her friends won't give up till they get it right!

#2 *Claudia and the Phantom Phone Calls*

Claudia has been getting some mysterious phone calls when she's out baby-sitting. Could they be from the Phantom Jewel Thief who's operating in the area? Claudia has always liked *reading* mysteries, but she doesn't like it when they *happen* to her!

#3 *The Truth About Stacey*

The truth about Stacey is her parents want to find a miracle cure for her diabetes. They're making Stacey's life so hard! The other Baby-sitters are busy fighting The Baby-sitters Agency. How can they help Stacey and save the club, too?

#4 Mary Anne Saves the Day

Mary Anne's never been a leader of the Baby-sitters Club. Now there's a big fight among the four friends. It's bad enough when Mary Anne has to eat at the lunch table all alone. But when she has to baby-sit a sick child with no help from her friends — it's time to take charge!

#5 Dawn and the Impossible Three

Poor Dawn! It's not easy being the newest member of the Baby-sitters Club. She's got three impossible kids to take care of. And Kristy thinks things were better *without* Dawn around. It'll take a lot of work to make things run smoothly again, but Dawn's up to the challenge!

#6 Kristy's Big Day

It's a big day for Kristy, all right — she's a bridesmaid in her mother's wedding! And if that's not enough, she and the other Baby-sitters Club members have *fourteen* wedding-guest kids to take care of. Only the Baby-sitters Club could cope with this one!

#7   Claudia and Mean Janine

This summer the Baby-sitters Club is starting a play group in the neighborhood. Claudia can't wait for it to begin — it'll give her some time away from her mean big sister. But then her grandmother has a stroke . . . and the whole summer changes.

#8   Boy-Crazy Stacey

Who needs baby-sitting when there are boys around? Stacey and Mary Anne are mother's helpers at the Jersey shore, and Stacey's mind is on hunky lifeguard Scott. Mary Anne's doing the work of two baby-sitters . . . but how can she tell Stacey that Scott's too old, without breaking Stacey's heart?

#9   The Ghost at Dawn's House

Creaking stairs, noises behind the wall, a secret passage — there must be a ghost at Dawn's house! The Baby-sitters find themselves and one of their charges wrapped up in a mystery. Will they be able to solve it?

#10 *Logan Likes Mary Anne!*

Quiet, shy Mary Anne has been growing up lately . . . and the Baby-sitters aren't the only ones who've noticed. Logan Bruno likes Mary Anne! He has a dreamy southern accent, he's awfully cute — and he wants to join the Baby-sitters Club. Life in the club has never been this complicated — or this fun!

#12 *Claudia and the New Girl*

Claudia really likes Ashley, the new girl at school. Ashley's the only one who takes Claudia seriously. Soon, Claudia's spending so much time with Ashley that she doesn't have time for baby-sitting — or her old friends. And they don't like it one bit!

#13 *Good-bye Stacey, Good-bye*

There are lots of tears when the Baby-sitters hear the news: Stacey and her family are moving back to New York. The club members can't think of a special enough way to send Stacey off. They want to give her much more than a party. But how do you say good-bye to your best friend?

#14 *Hello, Mallory*

Mallory Pike has always been good at baby-sitting her younger brothers and sisters. But is she good enough to join the Baby-sitters Club? The club members go overboard giving Mallory baby-sitting tests. Mallory's getting pretty fed up. . . . Maybe she'll just start a baby-sitting business of her own!

Bring home

New series!

SLEEPOVER FRIENDS

by Susan Saunders

Kate, Lauren, Stephanie, and Patti have great sleepover parties every weekend. Truth or Dare, scary-movies, late-night boy talk—it's all part of **Sleepover Friends!**

☐ **40641-8 Patti's Luck #1**
One night, Kate pretends to cast a bad-luck spell on Patti. Everyone laughs...until some *really* unlucky things start happening whenever Patti is around.

☐ **40642-6 Starring Stephanie #2**
Kate, Lauren, Stephanie, and Patti enter a contest they see advertised on TV. If they win, they get to star in a music video!

☐ **40643-4 Kate's Surprise #3**
The girls are throwing a surprise party for Kate. What a mistake! They have to keep all kinds of secrets from the Birthday Girl. Kate's not suspicious...she's just *mad*!

Watch for *Patti's New Look #4* in February!

Available wherever you buy books...or use the coupon below.
$2.50 each.